BRIDGE ACROSS THE SKY

Bridge Across the Sky

FREEMAN NG

NEW YORK LONDON TORONTO
SYDNEY NEW DELHI

Poems on pp. 1, 28, 44, 57, 58, 109, 135, 152–53, 175, 277, 334–35, and 342 are from *Island: Poetry and History of Chinese Immigrants on Angel Island, 1910–1940*, Second edition. Lai, Him Mark, Genny Lim, and Judy Yung, eds. © 2014. • Reprinted with permission of the University of Washington Press.

An imprint of Simon & Schuster Children's Publishing Division • 1230 Avenue of the Americas, New York, New York 10020 • This book is a work of fiction. Any references to historical events, real people, or real places are used fictitiously. Other names, characters, places, and events are products of the author's imagination, and any resemblance to actual events or places or persons, living or dead, is entirely coincidental. • Simon & Schuster: Celebrating 100 Years of Publishing in 2024 • For information about special discounts for bulk purchases, please contact Simon & Schuster Special Sales at 1-866-506-1949 or business@simonandschuster.com. • The Simon & Schuster Speakers Bureau can bring authors to your live event. For more information or to book an event, contact the Simon & Schuster Speakers Bureau at 1-866-248-3049 or visit our website at www.simonspeakers.com. • The text for this book was set in Miller Text. • Manufactured in the United States of America • First Edition • 10 9 8 7 6 5 4 3 2 1 • Library of Congress Cataloging-in-Publication Data • Names: Ng, Freeman, author. • Title: Bridge across the sky / Freeman Ng. • Description: First edition. | New York : Atheneum Books for Young Readers, 2024. | Audience: Ages 14 up. | Summary: In 1924 at the Angel Island Immigration Station, teen Chinese immigrant Soo Tai Go is awakened to the political realities of his new home as he waits to find out if he and his family will be allowed into the country. • Identifiers: LCCN 2023030620 | ISBN 9781665948593 (hardcover) | ISBN 9781665948616 (ebook) • Subjects: CYAC: Novels in verse. | Emigration and immigration—Fiction. | Chinese—United States—Fiction. | Angel Island Immigration Station (Calif.)—Fiction. | Angel Island (Calif.)—History—20th century—Fiction. | LCGFT: Novels in verse. | Historical fiction. • Classification: LCC PZ7.5.N53 Br 2024 | DDC [Fic]—dc23 • LC record available at https://lccn.loc.gov/2023030620

In memory of my sister Karen,
a family pioneer
in the studies of peace and justice

Angel Island has often been called "the Ellis Island of the West," but they could not have been more different. Rising near the Ellis Island immigration station is the Statue of Liberty, with its call to "'Give me your tired, your poor, / Your huddled masses yearning to breathe free.'"

Meanwhile, the Angel Island Immigration Station, along with the original detention center it replaced, were built to enforce the 1882 Chinese Exclusion Act, which largely halted emigration from China until the 1906 San Francisco earthquake and fire destroyed all of California's birth records. This opened up the possibility that an immigrant could gain entry to the United States by posing as a relative of a Chinese resident. Because there was no way for officials to validate these "paper stories" against existing documentation, they detained Chinese immigrants for periods that could run into months or even years while they checked their stories against the testimony of the residents they claimed as relations.

I. ARRIVAL

March 1924

As a rule, a person is twenty before he starts making a living.
Family circumstances have forced me to experience wind and dust.
The heartless months and years seem bent on defeating me.
It is a pity that time quickly ages one.

—Recovered from the walls of the men's barracks,
Angel Island Immigration Station

fallow field

I picture yesterday's river,
outside the village that was once
my home, beyond the grove
of dove trees with their long blossoms
hanging like wrinkled paper bats,
the river our parents
forbade us to swim, where we'd plunge
into the churn, blinded by cold
and the bright froth, propelling ourselves,
crossways to the current,
to rise, arms lifted, shivering,
on the rocks of the far side.

I hear our laughter
rising from streets we knew as well
as the outlines of our muscles,
where the old men and the married women
called out greetings for our families,
gossiped about our doings
and our futures, beneath
a morning moon.

I feel, still, the labor,
stooping, stooping, stooping
in the fields all day, the soil

drinking the strength
we'd carried from our beds,
but we knew
we'd rise with yet more strength
the next day and every day
that followed and that,
in due course,
we would harvest all:

A house.
A job.
A girl.
A life.

I should be there.

I *would* be there
but for my father and the plan
he nursed for who knows how long
before springing it on us,
on me, the day
I lost tomorrow.

(My friends
only envied me—*You're going
to Gold Mountain!*—when I
would have changed places
with any of them, except
that I would not have sent
my worst enemy into such
a dismal exile.)

I see,
I hear,
I feel
the cadences of a life
I thought would last forever
but that's now
forever gone.

Today's reality:
the line I stand in with
my father and my grandfather
and the other Chinese travelers
from the ship, this line
on the other side
of an ocean wider
than a thousand thousand rivers,
leading to the shut
double doors of the long,
squat building at the other end
of the pier, where we wait
to be told yet again
where to stand and when to move,
when to be quiet or to answer,
and eventually
whether we'll be admitted
to this country or sent back
to a land
I already mourn.

The doors
are opened. The line
begins to shuffle forward, toward
the dismal future I,

a good son, now
must hope for, but I'm thinking
of the *Jah! Jah!* of the magpies
that made their home outside
our kitchen window, of daylight
on a fallow field
in summer. Of Mei Ling
in her father's garden,
bending to pluck a weed
or caress the petal
of a flower.

faces

There were faces
of every shade on the ship,
some darker than ours,
some speaking languages that were not
Chinese or English. But only
the white ones
wore uniforms. Only the white ones
gave orders to the rest: *You there!*
Make way! Hurry along!
Stay out!

Father and Grandfather
call them "white ghosts." To me,
they are the pale powers. Ghosts
have the power only to haunt,
to frighten. These white faces
sit behind the desks
we line up at. They ask
the questions. They
guard the doors.

Grandfather sought them out
on the ship as if
they were nothing more

than fellow travelers, enlisting me
as his interpreter.

Where are you from? What is it like?
Have you been to many other countries?
What do you think of China?

Here
in the offices
of the pale powers,
in the hush
that fell upon us as we passed through
the building's double doors and
made our way to one of several desks
(the faces behind each one
impossible to parse for kind
or ill intent, though the interpreters,
Chinese, that sit to one side of each
seem friendly enough), he's silent
and bows his head, answering
their questions while swallowing
his own.

I hate them already.

When my turn comes, I look
only at my interpreter, rely on him
to speak for me. I'm suddenly afraid
to reveal my knowledge
of the pale powers' tongue, to invite
their special scrutiny. Even
in Chinese, I answer their questions
with the fewest words I can, once

with just a nod. Which
my interpreter translates as
Yes, sir.

Father
has no such reticence.
He greets them
like he's a visiting prince and they
are the escorts sent to receive him.
He starts right in, explaining
who we are and why we're here,
spilling everything
we have to say before
he's even asked.

Will it really
be this easy?

The interpreter doesn't pass
his verbiage on to the man
behind the desk, whose eyes
remain fixed
on his paperwork. Father replies
to the silence with another burst
of information, but the interpreter
interrupts him: *Please, sir, just*
your name and your age
and the village you come from,
for now.

The man behind the desk
doesn't look up, not even
at his interpreter. He only sighs

through his nose and raps
his fingers three times
on his desk.

Please, sir, repeats
the interpreter.

I look around
at the other white faces
behind their desks,
none of them turned up
to meet the faces
of the supplicants who stand
before them, and I feel
for the first time the weight, as heavy
as the exhaustion at the end
of a day of labor in the fields,
of what I always knew but only
as a floating, fleeting
technicality: that we might
recite our stories
flawlessly, answer all
their questions, pass
every test, and still
be turned away.

my story

I am Lee Yip Jing,
nephew of Thomas Lee,
a San Francisco merchant
with whom my father, his brother,
is a partner.

We lived together
in Kai Gok village, in the district
of Heungshan, in a house
on the northern edge
of the village, its door
facing south.

I shared a room
with my cousin Bing, who is
one year older than me, his birthday
on the sixteenth of August
of the Western calendar,
which is the only calendar
that matters anymore.

My birthday
is June 23.

Our room was in the back left corner
of the house. Next to it,
in the other back corner,
was my parents' room, with
my uncle's next to it.

My aunt's name is Shee Low.
My father is Wing Chi.
My mother, Lan Heung.

I don't
have a sister.

Our kitchen had
a small wooden table,
four chairs, an old style
brick oven with a grate on top
for cooking.

The house
had five windows, three
bedrooms, two clay dragons
flanking the entrance, which had
four steps and was exactly
seventeen paces from the road.

That is my story.

None of it is true.

Except for Thomas Lee,
a man I've never met
and who is not my uncle,

whose Chinese name
is Lee Kam On, who *is*
a San Francisco merchant,
who *does* have a wife, Shee Low,
and a son named Bing whose birthday is
the sixteenth day of August. Who lived
in Kai Gok in the house I described,
with five windows and four steps,
which was never
my home.

This
is our paper story, the lie
we must persuade
the pale powers to accept.

Who am I really?

It's best
not even to think it,
much less speak it aloud.

Or so
prescribed a tip
from a list of tips
my father bought
for a price
he wouldn't tell my mother.

this place

We sighted land. A new country
rose from the sea. The ship
crossed an expanse of bay wide enough
to swallow a district and its farmlands,
eased into port. But not
to let us off. The native passengers,
or those from countries
deemed acceptable, shuffled
down the boarding ramps,
a slow flow that accelerated once
it reached the docks and dispersed
in every direction. We remained
and thought, for a few frantic hours,
that the pale powers had ruled against us
in advance, that the ship
was going to take us back
to China. No. Another journey,
so much shorter and yet
just as far, brought us to this island,
to this cluster of buildings larger
than any palace and shoddier
than the poorest man's house,
to this room whose every window
is barred and every door bolted
from the outside.

I sit on a tattered bunk, one
among dozens stacked
three beds high and packed
so close, there isn't room
for two men to walk
between them. Clothing and towels
hang everywhere, and the floor
creaks constantly from the movements
of the men.

Why
am I here?
What will I do
in lieu of the life
I lost?

Father will not sit
but adds to the bustle
without purpose. He paces
back and forth, up
and down the aisles, exclaiming
to whomever will hear,

They pushed me! Did
you see it? They tore
my coat, right here!
What kind of accommodations
are these? To whom
do we complain?

The men who were already here
only nod or lay a hand
on his shoulder as he passes.

The other new arrivals
only look away.

I want to tell him
to sit down, be quiet.
That I heard—and understood—
what the guard who shoved him
threatened to do to him
if he didn't
shut up.

The English lessons
from my mother, unasked-for,
resisted, inescapable, have now
become a burden,
an entanglement. Knowledge
I don't want of a domain
I never sought.

That
your father?

A guy (about
my age?) plops down
beside me without so much
as an introduction or an ask
for my permission.

I grunt
my confirmation.

I could tell by how
you're looking at him, like you're

the father tracking
his overactive son, wondering
if you'd be more embarrassed
letting him go on
or reining him in
in public.

I can't
help smiling.

I'm Yuen Sow Fong,
he tells me, and I have to think
for a moment before replying
with my paper name.

He pauses a moment
himself before replying,
"Lee Yip Jing," huh? Okay,
good name.

He clearly
knows it's fake but seems
okay with it. He natters on.
I don't hear much
of what he says. Father
hasn't stopped complaining,
and he's now
working his way
toward the door.

I look
for Grandfather,
but he's nowhere

to be seen. He's wandered off,
like he constantly did
on the ship, another
"overactive son."

I sleep upstairs, but I like
to come down here to check out
the newbies. You probably
want to unpack and settle in,
but tomorrow, I can give you
the grand tour, if
you like.

Father
is pounding
on the door now,
calling out, *Hello?*
Hello?, and I make
to jump up and run
to him, but Sow Fong
stops me.

Don't worry. The guards
are used to this, and the others
will calm him down.

Men are gathering
around my father, patting his arm
and leading him away
from the door.

Grandfather
joins them, returned
from who knows where.

It never fails, continues
Sow Fong. *In every batch*
of newbies, in spite of everything
you must have heard
about the experiences of those
who came before you, there's always
one guy
who doesn't realize
that this place
is a prison.

a whiff

Sow Fong returns
to his upstairs dorm.
(My father gets itchy
if I stray too long.)
A pacified Father
finds me, and we find
our bunks. Grandfather
tells us what he found
upstairs: lavatories
and another room
of bunks.

A bell rings,
and the men begin,
in no hurry and with some groans,
to line up at the door of the barracks.
A guard yells, *Supper!*
and my stomach reminds me,
in strident tones, that I haven't eaten
since last night on the ship.

The grumbles increase
at "supper." Why are the men
so unenthusiastic

about a meal? Are they fed
so often?

We file out the door and down
a wide flight of stairs,
into a dining hall with rows
of long tables.

Newbie! someone
is shouting. *Over here!*
It's Sow Fong
at a table, waving
for us to join him—and then
to a man who almost
takes the seats
he's pointing us to,
Reserved!

We sit. I'm grateful
for the company
of a friend, however
provisional he might be.
He says, *Are you ready
for a treat?*

Bowls and platters of food
are set by servers
on our table. I learn
the reason
for the grumbles
at the dinner bell.

The rice
is a sticky, lumpy mess,
the vegetables boiled to the point
of nonexistence. The scraps of meat
are soggy, tasteless.

I'm seventeen years old,
and I'm in prison.

On the plate in front of me
is prison food.

Father
pokes at his portion.
He nearly spews
his first bite.

You won't *get used to it,*
Sow Fong cracks.
Quiet! a man beside him snaps—
his father, we learn—
and slaps him
on the back of his head.

Hey! gripes Sow Fong,
rubbing his head but with
a rueful smile. We sit in silence
and try to eat. Only
Grandfather seems content, methodically
shoveling mouthfuls and mashing them
between his few dulled teeth like a cow
chewing its cud. It's
the perfect food for him!

Prechewed and uncomplicated
by any flavor or texture he can
no longer detect.

Then
I catch it. A whiff
of something sizzling and savory.
A whiff of roast pork! Of *real*
roast pork, with crinkled, crunchy skin
over a generous
layer of fat.

Father
smells it too.

What is that? Where
is it coming from?

Sow Fong gestures
and we see: one table
is not like the others.
One table is decked out
with real food: the pork
we smell, steamed fish, gai lan
dark green and glistening.

That's
the Association,
he says. *But anyone*
can have food supplied for them
from the outside if
they have the connections.

I look around
and see a few other men
or groups of men with something special
on their plates, but nothing
like the Association's spread.

Some connections,
continues Sow Fong,
are better than others.

poems

A small piece of the sun
angles through the forest
of upper bunks to find my face.
I've been awake twenty minutes
but haven't wanted to move. Most
of the men are still asleep, or maybe
also stalling. The moment
my foot hits the floor, my day
will begin, and I didn't
much like yesterday.

Father snores below me,
but below him: the creak
of Grandfather pulling himself
out of his bunk, and then his face
looking up into mine.

Good morning, Grandson!

He dodders off
into the bunk bed forest (draped
with towels and underwear
rather than the dove tree blossoms
of home), and I shut my eyes,
letting my lids go red with warmth

that lifts me out of my bed, past
the ceiling and into
the morning sky, maybe
a sky with a moon
still in it.

I rise so high,
I can no longer hear the snoring,
or the whispers of the few men
now awake, or the creaking
of the floor beneath
their feet. So high,
I can look down, not
on the array of topmost bunks
that grid the room, but on
the living shape
of my village: the clustered homes,
the fields stretching their arms
to take in the countryside,
the pulsing vein
of the river.

Until a voice—
Grandfather's—rings out
as piercingly as when he first
spotted magpies in the tree
outside our house.

Poems! he cries.
There are poems
on the walls!

forgotten

There are poems
carved on the walls,
even at the height
of my topmost bunk, even
on the windowsills
and doorframes. There are poems
where poems have already been written
and faded with the years, poems beneath
the already old paint
on the walls. They cover
every inch of space so thoroughly
that up till now, I didn't see them
as anything more
than the mute texture
of the wood.

My reading is strong.
My mother also taught me
to read and write
our own language. My father
said it would be
important for business.
But there's a difference
between these foreign walls
and the neat writing tablets of home.

I do my best to retrieve the words
from the background layers
of history:

> *I have been imprisoned on Island for seven weeks.*
> *In addition, I do not know when I can land.*
> *It is only because the road of life has many twists and turns*
> *That one experiences such bitterness and sorrow.*

Seven weeks? Another poem laments that

> *. . . several months have elapsed.*
> *Still I am at the beginning of the road.*
> *I have yet to be interrogated.*

And another:

> *Today is the last day of winter,*
> *Tomorrow morning is the vernal equinox.*
> *One year's prospects have changed to another.*
> *Sadness kills the person in the wooden building.*

The bell announces breakfast.
Father calls to me to come.
How many meals
will we go to here? How long
before we're cutting our own poems
into these walls, replacing the faded verses
of the past, until our own inscriptions
fade themselves, are painted over,
overwritten, and they
and we
are forgotten?

unsmiling

I look for poetry
all the way
to the dining hall. It seems
to only exist in the privacy
of our barracks. No writing
in the dining hall, either,
or on the tables.

Sow Fong joins us,
without his father.

How was your first night
in Hotel Hell?

I survey
the men in the hall, trying to determine
from their looks alone how long
they've been here. One man's eyes
dart constantly, and he tugs
at the sleeves of his tablemates
with questions; he must be new
like us. A group of men
occupy a table, leaning back
in their chairs, holding forth
in turns with expansive gestures.

I imagine they've been here
long enough to learn all
of this place's ways
and to have an opinion
on every one.

One lone man
slumps in his seat. I watch him
for five minutes straight,
and he doesn't say a word
or take a bite of his food.
Is he new and overwhelmed
by his unexpected imprisonment?
Or is he the oldest
of the old-timers?

I think of the poems
of the men locked up
for weeks, for months, for
a year or more.
How will we look,
Father and Grandfather and I,
if we're still here
in a year?

Grandfather mentions
the poems.

Yes, says Sow Fong.
They're everywhere, aren't they?
I never had much use
for all that artsy stuff, but if

I'm stuck here very much longer,
I might just take up opera!

I ask him
how long he's been here.

One month.

Has he
been examined yet?

Oh, every which way—
you'll see!—but verbally?
Twice. The second time
went much better. I think I have
the Sè-less *Ones*
on the verge
of belief.

The *what* ones?
Father and Grandfather
stare blankly as well, but then
I realize with a laugh
that though this guy speaks
the same Cantonese we do,
he's made a pun
from Mandarin and English
(he knows Mandarin
and English!): the colorless—
the soulless—ones.

He means
the "white ghosts,"

I tell Father and Grandfather,
and they come out
of their confusion
sufficiently to ask him
about his examination, while I
continue turning
the clever compound word
over and over
in my mind.

Oh, they asked me
everything. How many rooms
our house had. What kinds of flowers
grew in the garden. How many
stars there are
in the sky. How,
after all, can you claim
to live on this Earth
if you can't remember
how many stars
are in its sky?

By the way, he says
to Father and Grandfather,
I'm Yuen Sow Fong—then
with a sidelong glance
at me—*and that's*
my real name.

Ah! says Father,
looking around and leaning in
to whisper to Sow Fong. *You're*
one of those who have

a real story to rest on. But Sow Fong
goes on in his speak-aloud voice
to tell us that the story he's spinning
to the authorities is as false
as anyone else's. *I just*
can't stand to use
a fake name when talking
to real people.

Has he no fear
that someone—say, a guard?—
might overhear his talk,
compare it with his testimony,
find him out?

Hey,
if they do,
they do. I'm not
going to live
in fear of them.

I gaze at him
in wonder. *So you*
know Mandarin and
English? I ask. *Hell, no!*
he fires back. *Well,*
some Mandarin, yes,
but only one word
of English.

Soulless, I say
in English.

A guard called me that.
I memorized it
and then waited for a chance
to ask one of the interpreters
what it meant. I wasn't surprised
when I got the translation.
It's what they think of us.
You'll see.

"You'll see" again. I ask him
what he means by it.

He shrinks, unsmiling
for the first time, into
a mumbling shadow
I have to lean in close
to hear.

Medical exams.
The Association
will brief you soon.
You'll see.

caged

The barracks
are a wide, two-story building
with long rooms of bunks,
we Chinese on one side
of the building, the non-Chinese
on the other. They're processed
much more quickly
than we are,
Sow Fong says.

When I first got here, their side
was completely empty,
and we were put in there at first
because the Chinese side
was even more packed
than you see it now. Their beds
are no better than ours, but then,
they don't have to endure them
as long as we do.

Each side
has a recreation yard. Ours
is fenced and small;
we can do little
beyond stand around in the sun

like cattle in a field, or under
a small awning like cattle
in a barn. We share
the lavatories, which contain
long rows of toilets
and a single long pisser
against the wall, unenclosed
by any dividers.
We sit or stand, side
by uncovered side,
and stare straight ahead,
no talking, even (especially)
if your neighbor is your father
or your friend.

The dining hall
is across the way and down
a slope. Between
is the stairway
we take to get there. Roofed,
with metal grating
on either side, it can only
be entered from inside
the buildings: a caged stairway
or a stairway inside a cage.

This place being
a prison, it must also have
trustees.

The Association
meet with us newcomers
in a room they use

as their office, kept empty
and off-limits to everyone else
in these overcrowded quarters,
and lay down the laws
of the place: no fighting,
no gambling, no theft,
no leaving a mess, no disobedience
to the guards. They might
be guards themselves,
the eyes and hands
of the pale powers.

They're like
our village elders,
only not so old
or wise.

Also: I
would never hope
to someday become
one of them.

the first thing

I shuffle along
at the end of a line,
a dozen of us led back
across the grounds.
I fix my eyes
on the back of the man
in front of me and feel
the eyes of the man behind me
on mine.

Will I cry?

I haven't cried
since I was six and hurt my foot
and my father took me
gently but firmly
by the hand and told me
I was too old to cry
any longer.

No one talks
on the way back to the barracks
from our medical exams.

We enter the dining hall
in order to reach the stairs
back up to the barracks. It seems
so small
when empty. Shouldn't it be
the opposite?

We gain the stairway,
and I begin to count the steps,
looking out at the bay
through the metal grating
to my right, trying to lose myself
in its vastness, to expand my spirit
faster than the bubble of tears
that threatens to burst
in the presence of the guards
before I'm safely back
among friends.

Father and Grandfather went
before me. They must be back
by now, returned
to find me gone.

If I'm able,
when I rejoin them,
to look them in the eyes,
will they look back?

Sow Fong
finds me first.

You're back! They sure
took long enough. Hey,
come here and look
at this.

He leads me to a window
with a view of the bay, babbles
about the time his family
visited some beach.

Can you believe
the weather here? Such a waste
to be locked indoors.

They marched us
to the hospital, into a room
with a row of screens, lined us up
in columns before each one.
As I got closer to the front
of my line, I saw more and more
of what went on behind
those flimsy barriers, but no sight
could prepare me, no briefing
by the Association (*They will take*
a sample of your blood
and your stool) could steel
my heart for how it felt
to be stripped
and scrutinized, pierced
by needles, made
to crap into a bowl.

Sow Fong is still on
about that beach. *Shut up!*
I want to growl, but then
he wavers, sniffs,
falls silent, and I realize
what my new friend
has been doing.

Some weather, I agree. *What's
the first thing you'll do
when we get out of here?*

both bigger

Jab the awl,
my father is saying, cheered
considerably by finding
a crew of cronies
to hang with. *Just*
jab the awl! he urges, telling them
the tale of the famed Su Qin—did he even
actually exist?—who failed
to win some job at the ancient court
and buckled down to study harder,
holding an awl above his thigh
so it would jab him
if he dozed.

Just jab the awl! Just
jab the awl!

I've heard that phrase
every day of my life and heard it twice
a day on the ship—it's what
my father says in answer
to anything and everything,
his creed and comfort—
but he doesn't have a word for me
all through the afternoon,

through dinner, and now
the shutting off of the lights for sleep,
this day
we had our medical exams.

I picture Mei Ling
in her father's garden, passing into
and out of the frame
of a window, walking down a street
ahead of me. I feel her
in my arms, her skin
I've never touched. My cock,
unfurling, frees itself, pushes up
through limp folds of clothing
and bedding, gets hard
and thick and right.

I don't
rub it out.
I let it go on pushing
against the world, imagine myself
in the examination room again, but strong,
erect, raising my arms as if
on the far bank of the river,
while around me, the pale powers
hunch at their desks, bent
over their own
wrinkled dicks.

Grandfather mumbles
below me in his sleep. He did
eventually find me
to commiserate over our day

at the hands of the doctors, but not
with his own words.

Grandson!
Come and see!

He dragged me
to a poem on the wall:

> *I cannot bear to describe the harsh treatment by the doctors.*
> *Being stabbed for blood samples and examined for hookworms*
> *was even more pitiful.*
> *After taking the medicine, I also drank liquid* [thymol or
> chloroform for deworming],
> *Like a dumb person eating the huanglian* [a bitter herb].

Strange
how this revelation,
that I only suffered
what many others already had
and would, made me
both angrier and calmer. My cock
strains against its own skin, both bigger
and more imprisoned
than before.

my heart

The house
of our village doctor was filled
with the dried-out smell
of root and leaf and twig,
or sometimes with steam
from the teas he brewed, bitter
with potency.

He diagnosed our illnesses
through nothing more
than his touch on our wrists
as we sat across a narrow table made
of a hard, lustrous wood carved
with designs of flowers
and dragons, fancier
than anything else
in the village, but whose fourth leg
was a plain wooden stump.

Sow Fong tells me
the exams we underwent,
the needles
and the nakedness, are just
how medicine is practiced here
and not some special torment

the pale powers reserve
for those they see
as livestock.

Not, he adds,
that they don't
see us as livestock.

I'm lying
on my upper bunk. We've been
to breakfast, but I came right back
and have no wish (for now
at least, I tell
Sow Fong) to be shown
any more
of the barracks or to go
outside.

Sow Fong stands
at the very end
of the bunk. His shifting feet
come close to tripping
over mine as he tests
how far along
the upward-sloping ceiling
he can touch.

Maybe it's for
the best, he says. *It's*
probably better,
right? I'm sure
we'll get used to it
soon enough.

I think of the man
who everyone
in the village, elder
to child, calls "Doc,"
my wrist on the worn
cloth pad he sets
on the wooden table
between us (the pad
that smells—I smelled
it once when he
was out of the room, holding
its softness up
to my face—like
the skin and sweat
of everyone else
in my village),
and he's asking me
how I've been eating,
sleeping, with utmost tact
how I've been shitting.

I tell him all, feeling
his fingers, soft
as a warm breeze, precise
along my veins, learning
all he needs to know
from the beating
of my heart.

here

Three days later,
I'm still in my bunk.
I go to meals. I go
to the lavatory. I have no wish
to go anywhere else. Sow Fong
hangs out with me
as much as he can, but he
has restless feet and can't
be cooped up
in the barracks all day.

I hear footsteps,
but they're not Sow Fong's
returning to make another attempt
at cajoling, nagging, or insulting me
into getting off
my ass. They're slow
and shuffling, a whisper
passed from bunk to bunk
until it sounds
below mine.

Grandfather
peers up at me.

Hello, Grandson!

I murmur a reply.

He turns
and begins to climb
the adjacent bunks!

Grandfather!
Careful!

He gets one foot
onto the middle bunk, one hand
on the top. His other foot
dangles.

Grandfather!
What are you doing?

I perch on the edge
of my bunk, ready
to grab him (and be pulled down
with him, no doubt) if he slips.
I debate scrambling down
to the floor, but he
might fall while I'm
in transit.

Grandfather!
Grandfather!

He's got the other foot
on the middle bunk now, both hands

on the top. He pulls himself up
to sit on the top bunk's edge.

He looks around.

The view is nice up here,
he says. *I see*
why you prefer it.

(*Ah!* I remember him exclaiming
the day he spotted the magpies
in the tree outside our house.
If only I could climb that tree
to sit and sing with them!)

Grandfather, I ask him,
do you miss the village?

Every minute, he says.
But every minute, I also fear
I'll be sent back.

Why? I almost shout. *We*
were doing fine. We weren't
like those other families
who had to try this place
or starve. Why
would we mess that up?

Grandfather is silent
for a long count. When he speaks
at last, he seems
to change the subject.

Did you know, he asks me,
that neither your father
nor your mother
wanted at first to marry
the other?

I did not!

She thought
he was too dull. He thought
she was too flighty. She
was always visiting
some far-off quasi-relation
on the flimsiest of pretexts.
The daughter of a fourth cousin
lost a toe. The nephew
of the village doctor
was getting married. Her parents
assured your father that this
was care for family that would find
its focus on him
once they were married.

He wasn't so sure. He was right
to be suspicious. I investigated.
I cornered her, persuaded her
to tell me the truth. She was learning
to read and write. In Chinese
and *in English! She'd hear*
about someone who could speak
some English or someone
who could read or write
in either language. Or best

of all, someone who owned books.
And off she'd go. She'd find
some branch of the family tree—
or if that didn't work, some branch
of a neighboring tree—that came
close enough for her to make
a double-purposed visit.

I instructed your father
to marry her. I assured her
I would support her efforts
to educate herself if she
would teach it all
to any children they had. Which
was her whole desire
from the start.

The interminable lessons. The burden
of knowledge I never asked for
and didn't want. They were all
Grandfather's doing. I feel
betrayed, more exposed
than ever.

Why?
I ask again.

Your father
is here to get rich. A goal
I support. He's doing it
for you and your children,
for the generations to come.
It's not enough

to be doing fine. The world
can change. A flood
can wash away the ground
you stand on.

Your mother is here—
in your person—because she longs,
through you, to enter
another world that can never
be washed away: a world of thought
and learning that will be home
to you and to your children
and to your children's children,
through all the generations.
I support that too.

Another set of footsteps
crosses the barracks floor.

Hey, newb! shouts
Sow Fong across
a mock expanse. *How's*
the weather up there?

Getting a little boring,
I tell him, and climb down
to the floor, help Grandfather down,
and then follow Sow Fong back out
into the small world
of our prison.

one day

There's a seven-foot man
among us. He has to duck
under doorways, curl
into his bunk. When he walks
around the barracks, though
the ceilings rise high above
even his substantial height,
he stoops. He never talks
except to mumble an apology
whenever he accidentally bounces
some skinny fellow inmate
into a wall or bunk.

Sow Fong says
the man's been here five months
but hasn't had a hearing yet.
He has no friends
that I can see. He eats alone
and quickly, never taking
a second helping,
though he must need more food
than the rest of us.

Some guy with a death wish
tried to fight him once, but he
just walked away.

Sow Fong scoffs
at both the foolish instigator
and his seven-foot target,
who could have flattened him
with a blow but didn't. I begin
to notice how, when the guards
herd us down the stairs for meals
and then back to the barracks,
or back into the barracks
from the recreation yard, they always
give the seven-foot man
a shove. I've gotten it too,
by chance like everyone else, but he
gets it every time, and sometimes
more than once if another guard
goes over to get in
his licks.

A man named Law Yen Yi
lays it out for Sow Fong and me one day
as we watch the seven-foot man
being ordered to pick up litter
in the rec yard that
he didn't drop.

That's what you call
a "sleeping giant." That
is what I call China.
The Americans, for the moment,

are more powerful than we are,
so they can torment us—
for now. But we are bigger.
We will grow stronger.
One day, we will wake up
and cross the sea in force
and destroy these barbarians.
I probably won't live
to see it. Maybe
you lads will.

what else

I find poem after poem
echoing Yen Yi's hope.
The walls cry out
for retribution
against the pale powers.

> *I clasped hands in parting with my brothers and classmates.*
> *Because of the mouth* [poverty], *I hastened to cross the*
> *American ocean.*
> *How was I to know that the Western barbarians had lost their*
> *hearts and reason?*
> *With a hundred kinds of oppressive laws, they mistreat us*
> *Chinese.*
> *It is still not enough after being interrogated and investigated*
> *several times;*
> *We also have to have our chests examined while naked.*
> *Our countrymen suffer this treatment*
> *All because our country's power cannot yet expand.*
> *If there comes a day when China will be united,*
> *I will surely cut out the heart and bowels of the Western*
> *barbarian.*

I don't have to walk
ten feet down a wall
to find more examples.

Someday when we become rich and strong,
we will annihilate this barbaric nation.

and

The day our nation becomes strong,
I swear we will cut off the barbarians' heads.

and

The low building with three beams merely shelters the body.
It is unbearable to relate the stories accumulated on the Island
slopes.
Wait till the day I become successful and fulfill my wish!
I will show no mercy when I level the immigration station!

As I read these poems aloud
to Sow Fong, I wonder
if there's a life
I might live here after all,
a cause
I can fight for in lieu
of the life I lost,
but he is unimpressed.

These guys
were just venting. What else
are you going to do
inside these barracks
with nothing to do all day
but fantasize about revenge?
Put guns in their hands,
and you think they'd be storming

the administration building?
They'd turn them in
to the Association in hopes
of getting favors in return. Hey,
I wrote a "fuck you" poem too!

How can this be,
when he doesn't know how
to read or write? He leads me
to another spot on the wall
and points. I see not a poem
but a picture . . . of a horse? *No, no!*
Below that, to the left.
Then I see it. The outline
of a cock and balls!

# of our own

I'm in prison.

Not just the prison
of our detention
but a prison
within this prison.

A prison
of our own making.
Or of
the Association's.

I find myself
in solitary confinement,
consigned here not
by the pale powers but by
our own Association
for breaking
Association rules.

My crime?
I wrote on these walls
that are covered,
every inch,

by writing. But not,
it seems, by any writing
not approved
by the powers
among us.

Did they really
tell us this rule
from the start?

The walls
are covered in poems.
The pale powers
don't even mind,
though I'm told
they paint them over
or sand them down
from time to time.

They never
made a rule against it
or punished anyone
for doing it.

That job fell
to us.

Sow Fong says, *Newb!*
I thought you knew! My
"fuck you" was a fuck you
to the Association!

My cell
is a storage closet,
or used to be, now
cleared out and used
by the Association
as their prison.
In it are a table
and a chair.
A bare bulb
dangling.

My sentence?
One day.
With bathroom breaks
and food brought in
from meals.

I really don't remember
hearing about
this rule!

We're ashamed, my father
told the Association
over and over. *You have my word*
it will never happen again.
Tell them you're sorry, boy!
Tell them I didn't raise you
to act like this.

Grandfather
only wanted to know
what I was trying

to write. I didn't know
myself.

Sow Fong
wouldn't stop laughing.

no wish

The walls
of my prison
within a prison
are clean.

I don't realize
the significance of this
until lunch is delivered
with the four-pronged utensil
we're supposed to
eat our food with.

I was caught
trying to write on the walls
with a nail I'd found.

I didn't think
to bring it with me.

I hold up to the light
the fork's sharp tines.

I know
the classical forms.
My mother

taught me.
Every poem
on the walls outside
is proper
in that way.

Maybe that's why
the Association
regulate it: to ensure
the forms
are followed.

I have no wish
to follow the forms.

I write a single stream
of unplanned thoughts
that doesn't follow
any rule. I write
in English, hoping
the Association
will see it as mere
scratches in the wood
and not erase it.

I start too low,
in one corner,
running myself
to ground, but carry on
the next corner over.

It seems like I don't
take a breath

the whole time
I'm working that fork
into dimly lit wood.

I finish well before
they come to collect the fork
and my plate,
still heaped
with food.

this poem

I just wanted
my life.
The home
I knew.
The people
I knew.
The work
I knew.
The girl.

The parental powers
said no.

I just wanted
to land
where I had to,
if land
I must, to open
the doors,
step out
beyond locks
and bars,
set foot
on new ground
beneath,

perhaps, a new
morning moon.

The pale powers
said no.

I just wanted
to write this poem
that was all
I could do
in the only
space
that remained.

The prison powers
said no.

My power
is a giant,
asleep,
undisturbed
by the shouts
of foes
or the mockery
of friends.

What will it do
when the time
comes at last
for its waking?

and see

They release me
at lights-out.
I go straight to bed.
I wake, still
in the larger prison
of detention.

Welcome to the outside . . .
inside, cracks Sow Fong
as we descend
the caged stairway
to the dining hall for breakfast.

What did you do all day?
Grandfather asks when we're seated,
but I'm not going to blab it
to Sow Fong and Father,
so I shrug.

Father spends breakfast,
all of the morning, lunch,
and the start of the afternoon
repeatedly telling me
you-know-what: *No more*
foolishness from you! We must
jab the awl. We must not anger

authorities of any kind.
We must work hard
and bank both our pennies
and the approval
of those above us.
This is the only way
to the security of wealth
and the serenity
of reputation.

Sow Fong asks
about jabbing the awl, and Father
tells the story.

Why "jab
the awl"? pursues
Sow Fong. *Wouldn't it*
be better for the student
never to doze off? Shouldn't
it be "Don't
let the awl
jab you"?

Father goes
silent, blank-faced,
at a loss
for the first time
in my memory. I seize
the opportunity to escape
to the rec yard, without
even Sow Fong
catching up to me.
I go straight
to the far left corner

of the yard, as far
from the barracks
as I can get.

I take
a long breath.

In the yard,
they're playing—
or trying to play—
a game we learned
from the Europeans
(whose rec yard runs the length
of the barracks, right outside
the windows of the ground-floor dorm),
played with a ball that's kicked
into a goal. But our yard
is smaller than theirs,
and more crowded,
and we suck, so our game
is a muddle of tussles,
a jostle of bodies
and kicking of shins
as often
as the ball.

I turn away
from the sight, look out
through the chain-link fence across
the wooded ground
that slopes away from the yard
and see,
for the first time,
the girl.

a story

Uh-uh, Sow Fong
is telling me, throwing
his whole body
into the shaking
of his head.

Nope.
No way.
Forget it.

I'm telling him
about the girl I saw, Chinese
I was sure, sitting on a bench
next to a guard, within sight
of the far left corner
of the rec yard.

What does he mean,
"Forget it"?

I mean,
she's Japanese! Or half-
Japanese. Enough,
in any case, that I
wouldn't touch it.

But what
is she doing here?

He looks at me,
screws up his face, and breaks
into guffaws.

You didn't know
there were women here?

Did women
make the crossing too?
There must have been
some. I must have
seen some on the ship.

I learn from Sow Fong
that women and young children
are housed in the administration building, and they
are allowed to walk the grounds, and this girl
makes a habit
of sitting each day exactly
where I saw her.

Didn't you know
they eat right before we do?
But that's as close
as you'll ever get.
So forget about
any of them, not just
the mixed one.

Half-Japanese. How
could it be? Which
was the Chinese parent?
I don't tell Sow Fong
any more about my sighting
of the girl. How she and her guard
sat with their backs to me,
how I watched them
for twenty minutes straight.
How the guard
got up to stretch and the girl
looked around
and saw me. How
she froze.

How we lived
a lifetime
in that moment. How I strove
to keep my expression
hopeful and open
and assured. How at last
she smiled back.

Half-Japanese.
I've never even seen
a full one. But there's a story,
from before I was born,
about a Japanese traveler
who tried to run off
with a woman from the village.
He'd lived for three years
among us, worked hard
and never caused trouble, until

his interest in her
became apparent.

He was warned
but one night
tried to leave with her
in secrecy. Or so
the story goes, and only
so far.

No one
would ever tell me
how it ended.

bigger

There is the rec yard.
Food you can have sent in if you have
the right connections. Even
a game room, such as it is. Too small
for the Ping-Pong table that sits
at its center and always crowded
by men gathered around
the Victrola (an invention
of the pale powers that,
I must admit, impresses me) or sitting
at two large tables, one
for mah-jongg and the other
for Go.

Some afternoons,
in the cacophony
of the game room like the noise
of an entire village packed
into a single room, I can almost
forget
this is a prison.

The Go players
snap their stones—*clack! clack!*—
onto the board. The Victrola

emits a constant medley
of unknown songs in strange
tonalities. The gang of fanatic players
who monopolize the Ping-Pong table
grunt and shout and send the ball
pinging and ponging (I grasp,
as sudden as a backhand cross-table rip,
the rightness of the English name for the game)
at speeds I never thought possible.

The mah-jongg players raise
the loudest din of all
as they scramble their tiles
for each new game, a sound
like rain, if the raindrops
were stones. They bang
their discards onto the table,
propel them into the discard pool
with a violence that increases
the more useless
the tile is. Their shouts of *Chī!*
and *Pèng!* when claiming tiles
to complete a set remind me
of Mother, whose voice
never rose as high as when playing
with the neighbor women
on the rare afternoons
when all the work was done,
with the old set of her mother's
that was missing
three tiles.

Whose voice
never sounded as soft
yet strong as on the day
I departed on this journey,
when she stopped me
at the door and asked, *You don't*
want to go, do you?,
and I admitted
that I didn't. She pressed,
Are you afraid
of the bigger world
you go to, or do you not believe
it will be bigger? And when
I found no words to reply,
she whispered/shouted,
Pèng!

here

I think
of my mother's
daily lessons, here
in this bigger world
in which I've (sort of)
met a half-Chinese girl.
After exhausting hours
in the fields, home at last
to wash the filth off, eat, and then:
my mother with her books
and writing tablets. *Do*
what your mother says,
my father would yell—and then
go off to bed himself.

My sister was the worst part.
My sister, Kow Loon. She was
the model student, always ready,
always looking forward
to the next evening's lesson,
though no one was forcing *her*
to take them. Always bugging me
to memorize and practice
with her, always
doing better than me.

I used to think, *What for?*
As useless as it all
would be for me, how much
more useless for her? Now
I think of my mother's quest
to buy my passage
into a bigger world. Is that
a thing that Kow Loon
hopes for too? For the children
she might have? I hope
Grandfather lives long enough
to ensure she's matched with a man
who'll let that happen.

I think of the girl I've
sort of met. Half-Chinese,
half-Japanese. She probably
speaks both languages. What
does Japanese sound like? How
is it written? How many
other languages are there?
How many lands, customs,
ways to carry on?

I no longer fear
the bigger world.

who says

The girl is there again
the next day, on the bench
with her guard.
It takes me two hours
after lunch to get free
of Sow Fong and work my way
to the far left corner
of the rec yard.

Will she turn around
again? Has she turned
to check already
and found me absent?
I'm gripping the mesh
of the chain-link fence
too hard. I settle myself
onto the dusty grass, where I
can seem to be watching the action
in the yard while sneaking
sidelong glances
at the girl.

I'm only able
to watch her for ten minutes
before I hear *TEEgee!*

bellowed
from the barracks.

It's the name
Sow Fong and I
have settled on for him
to call me, as he couldn't stand
using my paper name and I
couldn't bring myself to reveal
my real name to him.

T and *G*
are the initials of my name
as it would be spelled
in English, and I like
this new nickname. Once
I'm an American, it's what
they'll call me, those
who are closest to me, my friends
and business partners, maybe
the half-Chinese girl.

Teegee! blares Sow Fong
as he skips down
the barracks stairs, eyes locked
on my location in
the far left corner
of the yard. *Yo,*
TEEgee!

The girl turns
at Sow Fong's
jovial, annoying caw.

I stand.
I gesture
toward the yard
with a nod of my head
and a pat of my chest
and a shrug
to say, *That's me,*
T. G., he's calling for,
I have to go,
and smile.

She smiles
and waves hello
and goodbye.

I bless
the jovial,
annoying Sow Fong
as I hustle over
to rejoin him. How did I have
the presence of mind to play
his awkward interruption
so cool?

It was like
every tale where
the hero foils the robbers, outsmarts
his rivals, gets
the girl.

They say
that everyone thinks

he's the hero
of his own story.

Who says I can't
really be?

so began

I spend several days
trying to shake Sow Fong so I can go
to the far left corner of the rec yard
without revealing to him
my continued interest
in the half-Chinese girl.

Until she appeared,
Sow Fong and I were each
the only friend and occupation
of the other. Then, one day
in the game room, Yen Yi,
our expert on sleeping giants
national and individual
and a member of the Ping-Pong gang,
is standing at one end of the table
with a paddle in his hands
and no one to play.

Come on! he's begging,
hammering the air,
but he's finding
no takers. If he can't
for too much longer,
he'll have to give up the table,

perhaps to some pair of duffers
who'll make a sloppy,
unbearable
go of it.

The men at the Victrola, Go,
and mah-jongg tables
have seen and heard
and felt
the slams of the Ping-Pong fanatics
and want no part
of Yen Yi. I wonder
if I should claim the table
for Sow Fong and myself,
a small victory over, if not
the pale powers, then at least
the Ping-Pong powers.

Then a voice,
Sow Fong's, says,
I'll take you on.

Okay, kid.
I'll take it easy on you.

Do what you want,
old man. I might
surprise you.

Yen Yi never smashes
one of Sow Fong's
weak returns
like I've seen him do

to others, or hits any shot
with the pace or spin
I've seen him
routinely manage,
but he keeps it sharp,
and Sow Fong
stays right with him.
They punctuate
their rallies with cries
of *Weak!* and *Ha!*
and *Too slow!*

As the ball
and the smack talk
zip back and forth,
I see them not as projectiles
launched by one antagonist
against the other but as needles
stitching bonds
between a master
and his student.

Down 0–9,
Sow Fong catches the ball
just right, sending it
skittering
past Yen Yi.

Ha!
My point!

Well done. You could
be good.

Teach me!

So begin
Sow Fong's daily lessons,
an hour each day when I can go
to the far left corner of the rec yard,
a daily assignation—
wordless,
at a distance—with
the half-Chinese girl.

back

Hey, Boocher!
yells the kitchen boss.
Clear that table!

I get my first look
at the dark-skinned
kitchen worker.

How big a world!
is what Grandfather
murmured on the ship
at our first sight
of people like that:
two brothers from Ghana
in spotless black suits, lodged
in the upper decks, dark-skinned
like the kitchen worker,
though his skin is somehow darker
in his white kitchen smock,
surrounded by the white walls
of the dining hall.

The brothers were merchants (I learned
as Grandfather's interpreter)

with connections in San Francisco, but they
were not much liking America.

The crew,
they treat us like—
they treat us . . .
very poorly. Which
I was tempted
to translate, as I guessed
they meant to continue:
like you Chinese.

The kitchen worker
seems okay. He seems
about my age, way younger
than any other server
on the shift. He was
already clearing the table
when he got yelled at.
But the kitchen boss
yells again, *Come on,*
Boocher, move
that lazy ass!

The hubbub in the hall
subsides, converging
on a tone. Hard looks are cast
at the guy about my age
hauling a tub of plates
to the kitchen.

I hear "Black ghost"
being muttered, our term

(like "white ghost"
for the pale powers) for those
who look like
the kitchen worker does. I wonder
what other "ghosts" there might be
in our vocabulary, if everybody
not Chinese is some
kind of ghost.

Yen Yi, who sometimes
joins Sow Fong and me
at meals now alongside
Father and Grandfather,
though he never
speaks to them or they
to him, mutters, *Shit,*
he's back.

He tells us
that Boocher
worked here before,
but the Association
petitioned the powers
for his removal, which was granted
but now
apparently reversed.

I heard they just dumped him
on the women and the Europeans,
Sow Fong offers. *But I never heard*
what the problem was
with him being here
in the first place.

Yen Yi shovels
a load of rice
and wilted greens
into his mouth. Chews it
more thoroughly
than the overcooked mush
could possibly require.
Chases it with a swig of water
and a belch. Gives us
his reply: *Our ghost there*
is a spy.

a small book

Newb, the guy
is paranoid.

I'm surprised to hear
Sow Fong so contemptuous
of his Ping-Pong mentor,
but I agree with him on this.
Why would the pale powers choose
the most conspicuous person possible
to be their spy? But I'm not
really interested in the question. Instead,
I ask Sow Fong what he meant
by "dumped on the women."

The kitchen staff
works in shifts. All
the Administration did
was change his hours
to the earlier mealtimes.
Do you think
they'd really fire a guy
because we *demanded it? Hell,*
he was probably still working our meals
all the time, just out of sight
inside the kitchen.

He's there again
for dinner. The Association
refuse to let him set food
on their table or to remove
an empty dish. Yen Yi
grabs my arm: *Look there!*
You see? Boocher,
in a lull between tasks,
has pulled a small book
from a pocket. He's writing
something in it. *You see? He does that*
all the time. I believe
he knows our language.
I believe he's noting names,
fragments of conversations, so they
can catch us
in a lie.

What if
I cozied up to him?
I ask. *Maybe*
I could catch a glimpse
of what's in that book.

Smart thinking!
cries Yen Yi, clapping me
on the back.

Sow Fong stares
like I just sprouted wings
and a tail.

aback

I sit at the end
of the dining hall table
nearest the corner where Boocher
does his scribbling. Father
was shocked beyond words
when I told him, *I'm going to sit*
over there, as if I'd proposed
a murder, though it's not
like we even talk
when we sit together
at meals: it's always
Father and his friends
in one conversation,
Sow Fong and me
and sometimes Yen Yi
in another, and Grandfather
between us,
chewing.

I took
Father's momentary silence
as permission
while I could.

I do feel strange
away from them. Naked,
like when I stood behind
that flimsy screen
for my medical exam. A man
plops down beside me
without a word. Two
bickering brothers approach
and decide to continue their argument
in the seats across from mine. I look
to our usual table, where
Sow Fong is telling Father
some story that involves
elaborate gestures
and facial contortions.

Father is chuckling.

Grandfather
returns my gaze.

Boocher
carries out dishes, the kitchen boss
yelling at him continually,
though he seems just as quick
as any of the other workers.
When the initial service is done,
he heads as usual
for this corner, pulling
the notebook from a pocket.

Hey, I venture,
to no response. *Hey,*
Boocher!

He looks up
with a scowl I catch
in the moment
before he hides it.

Yes, sir? he says,
putting away
the book. *No, sorry!*
I reply. *I don't*
need anything.
I just wanted
to say hello.

Yeah? he says. *Okay.*
Hey.

I deliver the pitch
I planned, how there aren't
many others here our age,
on either side, so we
should talk. I tell him
my paper name, a little bit
of my paper story. I complain
about how boring it is
to always be sitting
with my father and grandfather
at these meals. I go on
about my paper village,
too much talk and more

than I'd planned, but when
I finally run out of words,
he chuckles.

Yeah, he says, nodding
toward the kitchen. *I don't
have much to say
to* them.

I tell him how I heard
that everybody our age
has to go to school here, and ask
why he's not there now.

Gotta work, he says
with a shrug. *But that's
all right. School or not,
you've got to
educate yourself,
you know? Make
your own way.*

I'm taken aback
by his answer, like one
that a village elder
might give.

He's called away
before
I can reply.

the difference

Our first month
in detention ends. We move
into a second. It's not
so bad. I've heard
how prisoners,
once released, can be so unused
to normal life that they yearn—
and sometimes
even arrange—to return
to the limited horizons
of their prison walls. We have
the game room, rec yard,
three meals a day,
however bleh. I have
the half-Chinese girl.

She turns
or gets up to stretch
at least once
every day. Sometimes
we wave. Her guard
never catches us.

Sow Fong says his Ping-Pong
is improving, asks me

to watch him play, but I beg off
in language that will provoke
a laugh but no
suspicion: *Track*
that stupid ball
bouncing back and forth
for an hour?
Go fuck yourself.

A new batch of inmates
arrives. They enter the barracks
wide-eyed, crestfallen
at the conditions. We say nothing
in response to their grievances, only nod
or lay a hand
on a shoulder.

Two men
are "landed"—a strange term
for being released
and allowed entry
into the country, as if
while in detention on the hard ground
of this island, we're still
at sea, adrift
on some frail raft
or treading water.

A third man
is rejected.

Men are called in
by the pale powers

to tell their stories.
We learn nothing
we didn't already know
about these interrogations,
nothing we haven't
already prepared for,
but each new cause
for optimism or despair
strikes us to the heart,
every time.

They asked
how many flowerpots
our house had. Who
knows that?

The interpreter
winked at me! A good sign,
right?

Watch out
for the officer
with the scar.
He has it in for us.

It was way
too easy! They hardly
asked me anything.

Three more men
are landed, after only
two weeks in detention,
and the comments take on

an edge of incredulity
and envy.

That's it? Your whole
paper story?

You have no friends
in power, here
or at home?

Help us understand
how this could be.

I talk more with Boocher, learn
that he lives with his father
in the nearby city
of Oakland, that he did
and still does
work the women's meal shifts.

I ask,
in discharge of my duty,
as casually as I can,
what it is he writes
in his book.

Nothing
to speak of.

Should I
pursue it? Do
I really care?

I tell him more
of my paper story,
good practice,
though Father already
quizzes me every night.
He tells me
that he and his father
moved here from Louisiana,
and before that, his father moved
from Georgia, new names
of places that to me
might as well
be on the moon.

I don't know how to ask
for the information
I need, that I've wanted
since hearing from Sow Fong
that Boocher works
the women's meal shifts.
That I have
no reason to believe
he can provide.

Could he even
tell the difference between
a girl who is Chinese and one
who is half-Chinese,
half-Japanese?

hell no

There are
so few of us, so few
our age, at least
on the men's side
of the station.
There must be
even fewer
on the women's side.

I simply ask Boocher
if there are girls our age
on the women's side.

Just three.

Where next
to go? How
to narrow it down?

He saves me
a second question.

One's half-Japanese
and catches
a lot of shit for it.

She sits outside
every minute she can, just
to get away from it.

Do the pale powers
hate the Japanese
even more
than they hate us? I'm sure
I've seen her and her
pale power guard
chatting like friends.

The guards? Hell, no.
The women. The ones
she's locked up with.
Her own people.
Yours.

what's obvious

Why do I feel accused
by Boocher's report
when I'm a guy who likes
a half-Japanese girl,
who is prepared
to not let that
deter me? While he busses
more dishes, I assemble
defenses of the women
in my mind but drop them
by the time he returns
and asks, *Did you have to*
leave a girl behind?

I think,
for the first time in a while,
about Mei Ling. The games
we played as children
when I'd always try
to be on her side. The time
we worked adjacent fields,
going up and down the rows,
and every time I reached one end
and turned, she'd swing back
into my view.

The day she started serving me
my tea herself when my family
visited hers.

I never
touched her. We never
walked together, talked.
But it's a small village,
and there were some
obvious matches.

What's
obvious now?

Boocher waiting
for my answer. I tell him,
No.

II. ACTION

At times, the barbarians would become angry with us;
They kick and punch us severely.
By chance, in their sudden cruel moment,
They would point their guns at us.
They scrutinize us like Prince Qin inspecting his soldiers;
They trap us with schemes like Han Xin's multiple levels of encirclement.
Brothers cannot share words, separated by faraway mountains;
Relatives cannot comfort one another, divided by the distant horizon.
Inside this room—
Neither Heaven nor Earth answers my cries.

—Recovered from the walls of the men's barracks,
Angel Island Immigration Station

okay

Talking
in the lavatory? I'm sure
I hear it, a murmur
rising and falling
like the flushing of the toilets
on any early morning—but this
is the late morning, when the place
is usually empty (okay, I've learned
to hold it in so I can come
when there's some privacy), and I hear
no flushing, true enough, but then:
the voices.

I think about the story
that's been passed along: the bride
who came to rejoin her husband,
who had a real, non-paper story
but was rejected
nonetheless and hung herself
in a shower stall.

The lavatory
is the place to "go,"
one man explained. The most
private place allowed to us, with pipes

running overhead both high
and strong enough
to tie the rope.

The women even now,
the man went on, *report*
strange noises
in the night: laments
and sounds of choking,
or they wake
unable to breathe, with a weight
of sorrow on their chests.

Nonsense! I think, then nearly
shit myself right there
when Sow Fong comes skipping
down from the room.

He looks almost
as surprised himself
on seeing me—*Oh, hey!*—
and hustles
right on past. *So!*
I think. *He likes*
to use the lavatory
when it's empty, just
like me. But when
I enter, I see several men
perched on toilets
around the room.

One of them
is Yen Yi. He looks me

up and down—so strange
to be measured like that
by a man with his pants
bunched at his ankles,
sitting on a crapper!—
and tells the others,

He's okay. You're
okay, right, kid?
He's been spying
on the spy.

I should have thought
to invite you in the first place,
he continues. *Come on in.*
But first, go tell your friend
to come on back as well.

ten minutes

If you had asked me
what I'd miss
in any prison,
I would have answered,
Freedom. But freedom
is the luxury
to plan, to act, to meet
the consequences
of those actions, wherever
you might be, whether
your doors open freely
onto the world or your windows
are barred.

The lavatory summit
runs for ten more minutes
after I return with Sow Fong,
who was stationed at the door
to signal the approach
of non-initiates—especially
Association—by walking on out
like he did. Ten minutes more
of the susurration I heard
from outside the room,
which turns out, from the inside,

to be a torrent
of proposals and debates
over action.

A hunger strike.
Petitions. The destruction
of furnishings or windows. Pleas
to landed authorities, to landed
Associations, to
the printers of news. Even
a call to violence
against the guards.

Ideas
are flung, praised,
excoriated, elaborated,
forgotten
and introduced again
with no memory of their history
in argument. All in voices
taut between
the speakers' urgency
and the need
to keep it down. All
in the ten minutes
they continue
after my appearance,
ten minutes of talk
so unlike
the usual sounds
of the place: the grumbles,
sighs, nostalgic reminiscence, even
the hopeful talk

of dim
and tedious futures.

Ten minutes of vividness,
of actions forceful
and outlandish. Ten minutes
in which the future
flips unrecognizably
from one declaration
to the next.

Ten minutes
that change the arc
of my story.

choice

They call themselves
the Resistance. They meet
in secret, passing word
of the next late-morning gathering
from man to man. Between,
they gather intel, compiling lists
of individuals considered
to be enemies: Bulmer,
the guard who clearly
hates us. The examiner who asks
the impossible questions.
The nurse whose blood draws seem
deliberately painful.

Boocher
the spy.

Yen Yi walks me
from the lavatory
through the barracks, an arm
around my shoulder. We pass
my father's startled
and then frowning glance,
Grandfather squinting

at some poem
on the wall.

Hey!
shouts Sow Fong.
How about
a quick game?

Yen Yi
waves him off.

We don't have to sit
like cattle enduring
their pens and their prods.
We can act, for ourselves
and our people. I might
get put on a ship
back to China, but those
who return on it
will fare better
for my efforts.

Light dawns around us as we pass
into the rec yard. A landscape
dawns in my mind, a possible future
of action for my people.

They stand around me
in the yard, grumbling,
sighing, waxing nostalgic
or hopeful. They only want
a life here: a job,
a house, a girl. Why not?

Why shouldn't they get
what they want, what
they probably
deserve?

The warmth of love
or the sun
leaves me weak-kneed.

What do you say?
Yen Yi concludes.
Will you be with us
or against us?

I had
no choice
about leaving home.

The only choices
to be made in detention
are which side of the bunk
I'll get out on, where
I'll sit at meals, how
I'll while away
the empty hours.

I tell Yen Yi,
I'm in.

thus

The Resistance
meets twice more
in the next two weeks.
I'm there,
sitting on a toilet
with the rest of them, my pants
bunched up around my ankles.

My need for privacy
is cured forever.
One day, I go ahead
and pee away and let
a big one drop, and the gang
erupts in laughter
far louder than any sound
we normally allow ourselves
to make, the first time
I've laughed out loud
so hard, with friends,
since I left
the village.

Sow Fong is there as well,
in his usual position
as the lookout,

standing just inside the door.
He never speaks but stays
at the door as we leave
to shake each hand—*Good meeting,*
good meeting—as we pass.

Outside the meetings,
I monitor the guards,
building our dossiers on those
who take the opportunity
to give an extra shove, to yell
without cause, who seem
by their aggressions
to be provoking us
to give them a reason
for more. I chat up
fellow prisoners, especially
the new ones, screening for those
who might join the cause.
I continue buddying up
to Boocher, now
with a double purpose: to hear,
as always,
what he can tell me
about the half-Chinese girl but also
to discern in earnest
if he's actually
a spy.

I ask him again
what he writes
in his book, as my father

across the hall
glares.

Nothing. Just
some thoughts.

I learn the name
of the half-Japanese girl—
Nakasone Yukiko Lan (strange
foreign names arranged
around the normal "Lan")—
and that her mother
is the Chinese one. I think again
about the Japanese man
who tried to make off
with a bride from our village,
the end of his story unknown
or withheld, and am glad
this other man
succeeded.

My father lengthens
our nightly paper story drills, adding
long lectures
on the importance
of discipline
and duty.

We must work hard
and follow the rules. We must
stay out of trouble. We must not
jeopardize our chance.

We must
jab the awl.
Do you understand
what that means?

I know
what he wants me
to understand. I do my best
to mis-
understand. I'm giddy
with Resistance.

Yes, Father. We must do
whatever we must do
wholly, with all
our will
and our strength.

One night, his attempt to break
his record for longest lecture
is interrupted
by Grandfather's stretching yawn
that ends with a groan
and an apology: *I'm not*
as spry as you younger folk;
please go on. But Father
can't, of course.

Thus ends
the lesson
for that night.

the whole board

Grandson!
Grandson!

Grandfather sits
at the Go board, across
from an empty seat.
Sow Fong has just begun
his daily lesson
with Yen Yi, and I
am on my way
to the far left corner
of the rec yard.

Grandson!
Come play!

He taught me
the game. I've always
enjoyed it. It's the thing
we do together.

I sit.

Six stones?

I nod.

I place six black stones
on the board, the advantage
I'm given to offset
his greater skill.
He makes his first move,
approaching my near left corner
with a white stone
of his own.

The game
begins.

I was on my way
to the far left corner
of the rec yard and then
to do more surveillance
of the guards and possibly have
a recruitment chat or two,
but I find myself relaxing
into the game, this reminder
of my former life
that was free of care and full
of humble hopes.

For the rest
of the afternoon, the battle rages
from one sector of the board
to the next as I strain
to hold back Grandfather's
relentless whittling
of my six-stone start.
Then we reach a position

where no more useful plays
are possible, and we count
the points.

I lose by five.

Good game,
he tells me. *You still*
need to work
on your vision.
You answer every threat
too automatically,
which lets me drive the action
where I will.

He lays a hand
on mine, pulling my eyes
from the stones
on the board.

You must learn
to see the whole board,
to not get so caught up
in local fighting that you miss
the bigger moves
that might be played.

It's what
he always tells me,
and I suppose
it's true. But I'm sure,
as always,
that I'll get him
next time.

an explosion

Father has discovered
there are Chinese newspapers
in the game room.
They're in big demand,
but he shows up every day
with his crew,
and the first one of them
who secures a paper
brings it to their circle,
where they pass it around
and debate its news
the rest
of the afternoon.

Yen Yi shows up
every day as well, goes straight
to someone with a section
of political
or business news, and asks
to borrow it.

They usually
hand it over, shocked
into compliance

by the boldness
of the imposition.

He scans it
quickly enough, thanks
the man politely enough,
returns the paper,
and goes on his way.

The world
is changing, he tells us
at our lavatory meetings. *And not*
for the better. We can be thankful
that in many respects our China is still
behind the times, that we still have space
to chart a different course. The pressures
are building, here
more quickly
than anywhere else.

Someday soon,
there'll be
an explosion.

into

How do you come
to the end of a rope?

One way
is from the ground.

The seven-foot man
with his head
always down, as if
to make himself smaller,
man-sized, ducking
the glares of guards and the stares
of fellow prisoners,
or as if unable
to look upward, onward,
to a future
he would never
reach.

Another way
is from the top.

He was called
for his interrogation
at last, two weeks ago.

Looked up then
from his bunk—a glance
not at the guard
who loomed above him
but at the ceiling, toward
the heavens, it seemed to me,
though I couldn't tell
if it was in hope
or resignation.

He pulled himself up,
head down again, and we
had no encouragement
to give him like
we'd given others, thwarted
by his difference
and his silences among us,
no pats of reassurance
that could reach
those mountainous shoulders.

This morning, his name
is called again, his fate
walked down
from the heights.

Rejected.

He does not lift
his head, not when his name
is called, not
at the pronouncement.
He sits on the edge

of his bunk, hangs
his folded hands between
the knobby peaks
of his knees.

Does he move
all morning? Another guard
with an interpreter
appears before him
with instructions:
what he must do,
where he now
must go.

Do you hear me?
Do you understand?

The interpreter
waits for a reply, bending
to look up
at the shadowed face
of the seven-foot man.
Finally explains
to the frowning guard,
He doesn't answer.

To us: *Will you*
make sure
he understands?

The lunch bell sounds. We flow
toward the door, a river

around the rock
of the seven-foot man.

I want!
The strong voice
we've never heard
halts us—*I want*
to write! He gestures
at a wall.

The Association
exchange frantic glances,
and I realize, *They're not*
going to let him! and feel,
for the first time,
rage. Not
at the pale powers
and their judgments,
not at the seven-foot man
for only now demanding
what he desires, but at
the powers among us,
within us, the old men
with their roast pork
and private jail.

But they say
yes! Or anyway,
one nods and the rest
turn away. The one
points out a stretch
of virgin wall, then
turns away himself. We

go on to lunch, the awful food,
the prods of the guards.
I chat with Boocher. Father
glares and frets. Yen Yi rails
against powers
of every kind. We forget
the seven-foot man,
a tossed stone
of misery swallowed
by our sea
of troubles.

How do you come to the end
of a rope? It takes
some doing. You have to
find a way to not
go to lunch when you're
the most conspicuous man
on the island.
You have to fashion rope
from torn strips
of your own clothing,
too unoffending to the last
to borrow any of the rope
from which your fellow inmates
hang their laundry, or to tear
the sheets or blankets provided
by your jailers. You have to break
the side-door lock through the force
of your own thrown body to find
a point of leverage—
the landing of the outside staircase
to the rec yard (not,

it seems, the recommended
lavatory pipes)—that can bear
your weight
and height.

A seven-foot man
with his gaze
finally lifted—past
the outside staircase landing
and into
the sky's clear blue.

the blue heavens

I, a seven-foot man, am ashamed I cannot stand tall.
Curled up in an enclosure, my movements are dictated by others.
Enduring a hundred humiliations, I can only cry in vain.
This person's tears fall, but what can the blue heavens do?

to rise

The seven-foot body
will be sent back
to China, as had been decreed
for the living man.

We all
had to pay for our return trips
in advance, the fee
to be refunded
if we're landed.
I never considered
the fare might be spent
like this.

We find his body
on our return from lunch,
blocking the view
of a first-floor dormitory window.
We find his poem
low on a wall
with all the space in the world
above it.

It takes all afternoon
for the pale powers to respond

to our calls, either
because of their usual habit
of ignoring or disbelieving
any complaint we make,
or because they are loathe
to face the consequences
of the way they treat us.
Meanwhile, we cut down
the seven-foot man
and lay him, not
in his bunk, but beside it
on the floor so that *for once,*
as Yen Yi puts it,
he can rest uncurled.

Yen Yi screams at the guards
who finally show up
to carry the body away.

Murderers! You killed him!
It was you! Sure as snow
in winter.

No one
makes a move
to quiet him,
despite the danger
he brings to himself
and to the rest of us.
He charges
the guards, coming
within striking distance.

They stoically
continue their job.

I want him
to stop, but I don't
want anyone
to stop him.

When the guards
have gone, he turns
on the Association.

You did this. You know it.
With your collaborations
and your capitulations.
Do you see what happens
when we will not fight?
Do the walls themselves
not speak of others
who have taken
their own lives? Will you
not speak of our history
in this land, of our people driven
from their homes, of the twenty
murdered in the night
within living memory
of some who sit here now?

Yen Yi stands
in a fighter's pose,
clenching his fists, facing
two Association members
sitting side by side

and looking not at him
but at a spot in the room
unoccupied
by any thing or person (unless
there's an ox in the room
that nobody else
can see).

The rest of the men
look away as well, each
at his own
invisible creature. Father
beside me goes further, turning
not just his gaze but his
entire body in the exact
opposite direction.

Grandfather
bows his head.

Among the crowd
of slumping figures, there's a subtle
shaking out: a man
discreetly stands, another
sets down his book
decisively. A coming
to attentiveness
by a few amidst
the willful ignoring
of the many, like the rippling
of tall grass
on a windless day
by animal movements

at the level
of the ground.

It's the Resistance,
ready to rise.

I rise myself,
limbs tingling
with the moment. Father
gasps and grabs
at my arm. I fight him
to maintain my stance, then catch,
across the room, Sow Fong
slouched against a bunk,
arms crossed, smirking
like this
is a comic play.

What's with him?

The dinner bell
tolls.

a roar

It begins
soon after the kitchen staff
starts bringing out the food.
The Association table
is served, and then
a few others.

I'm still
on my feet,
pursuing Sow Fong,
who's pretending
to look for a seat while really
running away from me,
while I'm being pursued myself
by Father, we
two hunters in pursuit
of an accounting
of a relationship
with the Resistance. I imagine
our first words, should either of us
catch his quarry, will be
"What the hell?"

Instead,
there's a crash

that's not
a dropped plate
but a bowl of rice
hurled
at a wall.
The soggy mass
has time
to slide only a few inches
before a bowl of vegetables
joins it.

The thrower?
Yen Yi,
standing tall, now
holding up
his plate.

Smashing it
on the table.

The Resistance
takes up the action.

More plates
are smashed. More food
is flung. A roar
goes up of shouts
and breakage.

I go cold, forget
about Resistance.
I would run
but for my father's hand

finding my arm with a grip
that tells me he's done
being misunderstood.

Sow Fong
turns, his face
grotesque
with fear.

I find myself.
Shake loose
from my father's hold.
Raise a plate
into the air. Bring it
crashing
down.

doomed

Twelve hours.

We've occupied
the dining hall for
twelve hours.

Dawn is breaking
outside
the metal-clad windows.

Twelve hours ago,
we stood together
against the guards' attempts
to move us back
to the barracks.

Then spent the night
in accusations
and recriminations.

You've
doomed us all!
We'll all
be rejected!

The many who joined us
in our action, increasing our mass
to the point we became
immovable,
have scuttled back to safety
in the light of day, reducing us
to ourselves again,
the core Resistance,
facing off
against the crowd.

Except
for the Association, who sit
at their usual table—did they
even get up from it
during the action?—with platters
of cold bok choy
and sautéed squid still on them,
not having spoken
a word all night except
to one another.

And except for Sow Fong,
who stands apart from every group
and pleads, *I'm not*
with them! I only
watched the door. I couldn't
even hear their talk!

Yen Yi glares, then stares
at him, then smiles,

then laughs (when I
can only rage) and announces
to the room, *Yeah.*
That's right. The kid's
okay.

sorrow

BANG!

A sonic shock
electrifies
the room.

Another follows:
BANG!

The barricaded door
cracks open, gapes, gives way
to a battering ram
wielded by a squad
of soldiers. Not staff,
not guards with pistols,
but helmeted soldiers armed
with evil-looking weapons.

We cry
in dismay, as one,
every man of us, including
the Resistance, no longer
an immovable object.
The soldiers surround us
in a second; I blink

at their speed. I look
for Yen Yi, but Father
is pulling me to Grandfather
in a corner.

Grandfather's face
shows neither fear
nor disapproval but a kind of
shy amazement, like the time
I took him out
to the forbidden river rapids
to watch me and my friends
brave the crossing.

But
Father's?

Not anger
or disappointment. Not
impatience, sanctimony,
judgment. A look
that makes me afraid
that he—or I—
will cry.

Could it be
sorrow?

my attempt

Did I once
nearly drown?

There was an afternoon
I slipped away to brave
the river rapids
solo. I remember
the bright froth,
the cold, and then—
not trouble, not distress,
but a floating, a vertigo
of velocity, and then . . .

I woke
in my bed, inside
the empty house, my clothes
still wet, my muscles
bruised and worn. I changed
but floated back
to bed. My mother,
when she found me there, asked
if I was sick. My father,
when I eventually rose
for supper, scolded me
for sloth.

Who saved me?

No friend,
no family member,
no other member
of our village
ever gave a sign
that it was them, so
I wondered—still
I wonder—if my attempt
to swim the river that day
had been a dream.

except

We're back
in the barracks,
locked down within
our usual lockdown:
no rec yard access,
our meals brought in,
the game room shut.

Examinations
are suspended; no one
leaves the building
for any reason.

Except
the Association,
escorted daily
to talks with the pale powers
they decline to share
the content of.

Sow Fong
is invisible. I make
no effort to find him. I spot him
once, in passing, on my way
to the lavatory, sitting on a bunk

in the upstairs quarters
while his father rails at him,
smacking
the back of his head.

My own father remains
immersed
in silence. He won't speak
even to scold.
I try to stay by him,
eating my meals by his side.
I want to tell him, "Keep
jabbing the awl!" except
I can't think how
it wouldn't be heard
as mocking.

Grandfather
circles the walls, reading
and rereading the poems, like a bird
trying to find the window
out of a house it entered
by mistake. He drags me along
some days, a grand tour
of hopelessness.

> *My life at an impasse, I left house and home;*
> *I braved the winds and broke through waves to cross the seas.*
> *Yet with one wrong word, my bridge across the sky was broken;*
> *Now I've been imprisoned for two years in a wooden building.*
>
> *It's hard for heroes to cross the barrier to America;*
> *Both going forward and back are hard, and in the quiet night*
> *I sigh.*

I leave behind this floating life—there's only one road for me now;
My wronged soul is doomed to wander—what else can I do?

"My bridge
across the sky."
For the first time, I'm struck
by the poetry of the poems
on the walls. The Resistance
was my bridge
across the waters, the future
I could live. A bridge now
in shambles, rubble
borne away by the
vertigo of velocity
between the near shore
and the far.

Yen Yi
begins to rally.

We weren't wrong, he tells me
and anyone else
who'll listen. *We couldn't go on*
the way we were. Our jailers
needed to hear us shout it. Why
is this even a jail?

He tries to organize
another lavatory meeting
of the Resistance.

I doubt
that many will show.

the thick of it

The Resistance
is escorted
to the dining hall.

The Association
are already there,
sitting at their usual table,
but all on one side, not diners
but a panel
of judges.

Guards
surround the space, but there
are no soldiers
in sight.

What can they do?
argues Yen Yi. *They can't*
squeeze us all
into their little
one-room prison.
Will we go
in shifts?

They can see
we are deported!

one man hisses,
and Yen Yi cringes
and goes silent.

To my own surprise, I come
to his defense.

Then maybe those
on the next ship from China
will fare better
for our efforts.

That's right,
says one man. *Good call,*
another quietly tells me. A third
says, *That's absurd! What good*
can come to anybody
out of this?, staring me down as if
I were a grown man
like the rest.

I make
an answer, am answered
in turn. A standard
Resistance debate
ensues, with me
right in the thick of it.

Through all
of it: Yen Yi's
undying
smile.

satisfaction

Gentlemen,
begin the Association.
Please pass this news
to the others, who will be joining us
shortly for lunch. (I realize
the tables are indeed set up
for a meal.) *Within a few weeks,*
the meal budget will be increased
by five cents per man, the menu
will be diversified, and more cooks—
Chinese—will be hired
to do the cooking. In addition,
a concession will be opened
where we can purchase
sandwiches or snacks
to supplement
our diet.

A few of us
goggle in wonder
but are woken
by Yen Yi's roar:

You turned our action
into a tantrum

over food? Do you think
the man who killed himself
could not go on
because the rice
was soggy? Or is
your own comfort
so important to you
that his death
was lucky currency
that fell
into your hands?

We shout
our agreement,
united again.
The Association
fix their eyes
on the invisible ox
once more
in the room.

The silence
lengthens. We
can wait them out.

They speak.

Finally, within
those same few weeks,
the following station staff
will be removed
or replaced.

They proceed to call a roll
that might have come
from our own list
of enemies. Bulmer
the belligerent guard, the clumsy
or pernicious nurse,
the unfair examiners.
They cover half our list
and add a few names
we never had. (Not
Boocher's, though.)

When they are done,
they don't so much as smile
in satisfaction
at our open-mouthed
amazement.

Footfalls sound
on the stairs from the barracks.

Why don't you join
the others now? (Law Yen Yi,
will you remain
a moment?) They will soon
be here for lunch.

Please remember
to give them the news.
We thank you
for your assistance.

a salute

They stole
our thunder! We
took the risk, and they
stepped in
like heroes.

They did
the right thing. What more
could we ask?

They could have
done more.

They could
have sold us out.

We don't know what to make
of the Association's turn.
We'd look to Yen Yi
for the correct
interpretation, but he's still
at the Association table,
shaking shaking shaking
his head.

The others
are entering the hall,
and I need to find Father
and Grandfather, and need
to stay with the group
and work out
what just happened,
and need to hear from Yen Yi
what he's so adamantly refusing
or denying
to the Association.

Father and Grandfather
appear at the door. My decision
is made. I tell a Resistance man,
I'm going to tell my father
the news, and run to meet them.

Father
hugs me! (If he ever
did before, I must have been
so young, I can no longer
remember it.) I tell him,
I'm all right. I tell him, *We're*
all right. I tell him
our action succeeded,
that the powers agreed
to remove the worst
of the staff and promised
to improve conditions.

I have to help him
into a chair. Grandfather

resumes his look
of befuddled admiration.

We sit and eat, surrounded
by a heightened buzz.
I see members of the Resistance
going from table to table,
spreading the news
and perhaps our debates
over the news. The food,
though it's the same
awful stuff, somehow
tastes better, the way
it soon will. Yen Yi is still
at the Association table,
sitting. They're all
sitting now, around
the table, diners
once more.

Boocher
is trying to catch
my attention. He's smiling
and waving me over
like a kid. I shrug
and gesture: *I'm stuck
with family.* He starts
walking toward us but retreats
at my father's
upturned glare.

Lunch ends.
We head for the stairs.

Yen Yi is still
at the Association table.
Boocher, clearing some dishes,
sees me looking his way,
sets down his load,
and pulls himself, beaming,
to attention. Raises
a closed
but outward-facing fist.

I take it
as a salute
and return it.

the moment

The third month
of our detention
is a golden age. The food
gets better. Not close
to what can be brought in
if you have
the right connections—that mark
of privilege undisturbed
by any upheaval—but the meats
find a middle ground
between soggy and incinerated,
the vegetables are baked or sautéed
instead of being uniformly boiled,
and individual grains of rice
can sometimes
be discerned.

The guards and staffers
the pale powers agreed to remove
disappear
within a week.

No punishment—
or praise—comes down
from the Association
for any Resistance member,

though Yen Yi
is frequently called to their office
for discussions he declines
to share the content of.

The others
call out our names
and slap our backs
whenever we pass, to the point
that I wonder
if Sow Fong regrets
his abandonment
of the cause. I bump
into him constantly, weirdly
way more often than when
we hung out together, but
we never say a word
in passing. I had to leave
my friends already, once,
when I left my village, but that
was not my fault.
I would have stayed
but was forced to go.
Same now, I tell myself. *He*
forced the parting. He's
the one who chickened out,
aligning himself
with the complacent,
cowardly crowd
of the occupied dining hall.

A reporter
from one of the game room

Chinese newspapers
shows up and spends
an entire afternoon
in the Association office,
hearing from them
and Yen Yi
about our action
and the conditions
of our imprisonment.

Father
goes silent, even ceasing
our daily paper story drills.
Grandfather sits
or walks with him, talking,
I assume,
about the problem
of me: radical,
victorious
me.

Boocher
seeks me out
continually, Father
no longer blocking
his approaches, the Resistance
happy to let me continue
my interrogation
of the suspected spy.

You did it, man! You
did it! You made
change happen.

Not realizing
that one change
we failed to effect
was his removal.

How did you plan it? What
were the factors, the options,
the goals?

Is he
indeed
a spy?

I have
no secrets
to spill. *We didn't*
plan anything.
We talked a lot, but it
just happened.

He nods
as if at some
great wisdom.

Maybe that's how
it works. You talk,
you plan, you
yearn, you endure.
Then the moment—all
on its own, it will seem—
arrives.

from rubble

I lie in my bunk,
unable to sleep
yet again. I've gotten
so little
since the day of the action
in the dining hall, awake
through that night and far
into subsequent nights,
from worry at first
and then
in celebration, unwilling
for the waking hours
of these triumphant days
to end.

I imagine
San Francisco ablaze
with the fire that followed
the earthquake, that made
our entry possible
by destroying the records
of businesses and births,
by wiping clean
the slates on which

we're writing
our new stories.

I imagine
the fire burning on
from city to city
across this land,
the world, consuming
all of the past,
the ancient hatreds,
fears.

A world
broken
and then burned.

I lie in my bunk, unable
not to dream
of the new world rising
from rubble and ash, in the light
of bright days to come
and the moonlight
faint
through the windows.

blank

I'm checking in
on all the rooms on my way
to the far left corner
of the reopened rec yard.
Father and Grandfather
sit on Grandfather's bunk.
Father turns away
when he sees me. Grandfather turns
to look in my direction. A man
calls out, *Thank you!*
and toasts me
with his purchased sandwich.

I enter the game room, bask
in the restored din
of mah-jongg tiles and cursing, the snap
of Go stones, the song
of the Ping-Pong ball
as Yen Yi rallies—
with Sow Fong! He's playing
Sow Fong. They're laughing
and exchanging insults.
Members of the Resistance
dot the crowd that cheers
them both.

Good shot!
cries Yen Yi at what
must have been
a good shot. Sow Fong
beaming and strutting until
he sees me watching,
and his face
goes blank.

always

When I get
to the far left corner
of the rec yard,
the half-Chinese girl
is on her bench, looking
right at me. She sits
beside her guard
but twisted around to gaze
quite frankly
toward this spot. Has she
been waiting, all this time,
for my return?

She smiles.

A smile
just as big
takes hold of my face,
as if the corners of my mouth
were pulled
by invisible strings
connecting them
to hers.

Then I know it:
I will find a way
to speak with her.
Because action
can change the world, luck
is bestowed on the bold,
and the moment
always arrives.

III. BETRAYAL

Living at home, there were no prospects for advancement.
The situation forced one to go to another country.
Separated from the clan, a thousand miles away,
Apart from the ancestors, we are no longer close to one another.

—Recovered from the walls of the men's barracks,
Angel Island Immigration Station

to face

She turns
to face away again, seated
beside her guard. I turn—
to face
Sow Fong.

*So you're into her
after all!* he cackles.
I can't blame you.

He stands there
grinning. It's hard
not to smile back.

I manage it.

Because, he presses,
*I'm a coward. Right?
I couldn't do
a brave thing if my life
depended on it. Or EVEN
a girl.*

I face him,
silent. His grin subsides
into a grimace.

Anyway,
he says, a new,
wan smile
on his face. *You're*
the one with the guts.
You're the one
who did his duty, the spying,
and the recruiting,
and everything else.
You joined the riot
when they could have
bashed your skull.
And in the end,
you won. You all did.

I bet you'll win
the girl, too.

He turns
to go.

It's funny
how the happiness
of hope can light
a whole house
of darkened rooms.

Hey! I call.
I gesture toward
the half-Chinese girl.
Wanna hear
about it?

that smirk

I tell Sow Fong
about my encounters
with the half-Chinese girl.
The glances. The glances. The
glances. It doesn't
amount to much.

It's awesome!
he counters. *You broke through*
the walls. You slipped
through the bars, if only
with your eyes
and your heart.
It's practically
a miracle!

I tell him
I want more
than a miracle.

What about
Boocher? he continues
brightly. *Couldn't he*
pass her a note?

Boocher.
Who serves
both meal shifts.
Who knows who
the girl is.

I'm already composing the note
I'll ask him to pass her
as I ask Sow Fong
about Yen Yi.

He's cool. We're
cool. Whether
it's Ping-Pong
or politics,
he's basically
a fanatic. As long
as I keep up
my Ping-Pong improvement,
he'll be
okay with me.

I tell him
he can improve in Yen Yi's eyes
politically
as well, that there are sure
to be further actions, that he'll have
more chances to prove
his worth.

He takes
a step back, hands

on his hips, that smirk
back on his face.

Not likely,
my friend. Not
likely.

hope

To Nakasone Yukiko Lan,

I don't know how to write
the Japanese parts of her name except
to spell out their sounds
in English. The rest
I write in Chinese, as my English
isn't good enough to express
all that I might someday
want to say, and anyway,
Chinese is the language
she'll most likely find help
to read.

I hope
this letter
reaches you.

I'm the guy
who waves to you
from the Chinese rec yard.

I'm here
with my father
and grandfather.

We come
from Kai Gok village.

I hope

I pause
in the writing, unsure
of what I hope for.

I wish, I might once
have written, *that I*
had never been dragged
from my home. Is that
still true?

I hope
you have been comfortable
in your confinement.
Our present conditions
are difficult, but I believe
there are better days ahead
for all of us.

I imagine Boocher
handing her the letter. Will she
be apprehensive
at being approached
by the dark-skinned
kitchen worker?

You can trust the person
who will deliver this to you. We're friends,
and he's happy to help and to carry

your reply, if you care
to make one, back
to me.

Yours
in detention,

Lee Yip Jing

the notes

I wait for Boocher
at the next meal. My letter
is sealed in an envelope with only
my paper name on it so that in case
it miscarries, there's a chance
it will be returned to me
without its contents
being read. I feel conspicuous
just sitting there with it
folded in a back pocket, as if
everyone—the prisoners, the staff,
the guards—can see the mark
of its rumpled outline
on my ass.

Boocher passes close
a couple of times
but veers away, the kitchen boss
driving him to table after table
before he can retreat
to this corner, where
he takes his breaks.

And then he's here.

Hey, Boocher. You serve
the women's meal too,
right? He nods, his eyes
focused on what he's writing
in his notebook. *You know*
the girl? You know—Yukiko?
The girl who's half-Japanese?

He puts away the notebook, turns
his full attention to me.

I wrote a note. To her.
Can you deliver it?

His eyes widen,
narrow, dart
across my person
like he's trying to discover
where I have it. I suppress an urge
to cover my pocket
with a hand. I want to tell him,
Look away! Don't
draw attention!

If it's too much trouble . . . ,
I begin. Even as I scream
to myself, *Just shut up*
and let him answer!

He answers no.
It probably would
be a little too much.
Trouble, you know?

Still yelling at myself
that I'm a wimp, I tell him
that I understand. That I can see
how he would get
in so much more trouble
if he were caught
than any other kitchen worker.
That I can just as easily
ask one of them, if he could help me
find someone who also serves
both meals.

He pauses, biting
his lip. *Naw, no need*
for that. I'll do it. I'll take
your letter.

I want to jump
right out of my chair
and hug him. I feel
I've made a second friend.

You're sure
it's okay? I ask. *You won't*
get in trouble
if you're caught?

Oh, he replies, *I'd get*
in all manner of trouble.
But look around you.
There are more notes
being passed at meals

than on Christmas Eve
at the post office.

I do
look around.
But have no idea
what he means.

You don't know
about the notes?

He tells me that notes
to help us with our interrogations
are smuggled in by kitchen staff
who live on the mainland.
That from there, they go
to the Association's table.

The Association?
Breaking the rules
of the pale powers?

It's safest
and easiest
that way. They
make sure the notes
get to the ones
they're meant for,
in the privacy
of your barracks.

Is Boocher
part of this network?

Hell, no! They'd never
trust me. They don't
even know
I know.

I lie awake
that night, thinking
of my letter
in Yukiko's hands,
of everything
I'd thought or assumed
about the Association, and of
my new certainty
that Boocher
is no spy.

its places

Yen Yi finally calls
another meeting
of the Resistance.

Others
want to join us,
but Yen Yi is firm
that this meeting, at least,
will be the core Resistance
only.

We all agree.
We took the risk. We won
the victory, however
the Association
might spin it. We
should have the chance
to celebrate among ourselves
before we expand
the movement.

This time, though,
there's no need
to squat in secret
in the upstairs lavatory.

This time,
we've reserved
the game room, and not
a single fellow prisoner, not
the Association themselves,
objected.

I sit
at the Go table,
fingering the stones.
Yen Yi stands
at a familiar spot at one end
of the Ping-Pong table. Others
are still filing in, and through the door
I see Sow Fong's
approach.

What
is he thinking?

He reaches the door
and stops, turning
to lean up against the frame, apparently
on watch again, as if nothing
has changed. I can't
stop staring. Yen Yi catches me
staring, turns, and spots
Sow Fong.

Hey, kid! he yells.
Come on in! No more need
for a lookout, right?

Everyone
seems okay with this,
and I'm happy
for my friend.

So, begins Yen Yi. *We did it.*
We showed our jailers
that we are men
who cannot be treated
like cattle. We showed
the Association that action,
direct and extreme,
has its proper times
and places.

There are cheers
all around, but "has
its proper times and places"
doesn't sound entirely
like Yen Yi.

In fact,
the Association
have been very much
persuaded. Enough
that they're considering
other actions, pushing back
against the Administration
far harder than they have.

The cheers
continue, mounting
with every line.

Enough
that they actually
want to work with us. Enough
that they've asked me
to join them.

Silence.

I see my own shock
reflected
on every face.

I know, says Yen Yi, shifting
to a gentler tone. *I know.*
It seems incredible. It might even
seem traitorous. But listen . . .

He goes on
talking. I fix
on Sow Fong's face,
the only face
in the room still
smiling.

either

It's dinner
and across the room,
Yen Yi sits at the Association table,
scrutinizing a dish piled high
with chunks of roast pork,
chopsticks hovering
like the claws
of some bird of prey
poised
for acquisition.

He talked his way
out of trouble at the big
Resistance meeting.
Everything he said
in the game room
was true.

What
did "Revolution" mean
if not the changing
of men's minds?

Who were we
to reject the changing

of the Association's
collective mind?

How much good
could he—could we all—
do, with the leverage of his
new placement?

Another member
even pointed out
the Association's work
to smuggle cheat notes
into the barracks, a fact
I'd only just learned
from Boocher.

But then how could they—
how could Yen Yi—
previously speak
of the Association, the men
Yen Yi is supping with
right now, as pure evil
when all the time they also knew
this fact?

Boocher walks by,
and I forget about Yen Yi.

*Hey, Boocher! Were you able
to get her my letter?
The girl?* He flinches, as if
at an unexpected blow. His eyes
survey the room like he'd rather
be anywhere else.

My spirit falters. I know
he's steeling himself
to deliver bad news.

But he says, *Yeah.*
She got it.

I begin to rise
from my seat to thank him
(to shout, to dance
a jig), but he presses me
back down.

Look, he says. *Don't*
get your hopes up.
Okay? She might freak
over someone sending
her notes. She might
already have a guy,
you know? Back home.

He's right, of course.
Though I only wanted
to send her a note, who knows
for what? Of course he sees
what I was really hoping for.
He's a guy, after all,
like me.

Yen Yi is making
some emphatic point
to the Association,
jabbing at the air

with his chopsticks. Everyone
is smiling. *There,* I think
to myself, *is a man*
who got everything
he wanted. So such a thing
is possible. The rule
seems to be that it will always
be someone else.

Boocher sees me
looking that way.

That's the leader,
isn't it? Of your Resistance.
What's he doing
there?

I tell him
everything.

That's how
it goes, he says.
There are no
bad guys or good guys.
There are *bosses*
and workers, and a man
can be both.

But either,
boss or worker, friend
or foe, can both help you
and betray you.

everybody

Yen Yi's ascension
scrambles the routines
of many.

Father resumes
our nightly paper story drills
without a mention
of why we stopped
or even
that we stopped.

Grandfather
joins the Resistance but only
in the new form it takes: tiers
of advisory committees
through which
petitions and suggestions bubble up
until they reach
the Association table.

Half the men are engaged
at one level
or another.

Not me.

I doubt
Yen Yi even knows
that I'm no longer
part of the group.
He's surrounded
every moment
by admirers,
a mother duck trailed
by its chicks, a nursing pig
with a litter
at its teats.

The Association
organize lectures
at which Yen Yi holds forth
on Chinese history
and our history
in America.

Sow Fong
attends the lectures,
comes back to me
with innocent reports
of facts he learned
as if they're details
of some song
or fairy tale and not
the grim truth
of our world.

Did you know
we helped them build
a railroad that stretches across

their entire country
as wide as China, but now
that it's done, they want us
out of here? So clever,
don't you think?

Just like how Japan's
been pushing us around
for decades. Did you
know that? You really
have to tip your hat
to them; they beat us
every time.

Of course I knew
about the Japanese. How
did Sow Fong *not*
till now? And if
he didn't know it . . .

If you didn't know
our history with Japan,
then why were you so opposed
to the girl?

Give me some credit,
Sow Fong sniffs. *I don't*
have to know someone's
the Enemy to know
someone's the Enemy.

Okay, I counter, *how* do
you know someone's
an enemy?

Everybody, he says
like it's a punch line,
is the Enemy!

he informs me

Sow Fong sits with me
in my vigils over Yukiko.
He's been abandoned
by Yen Yi, who has
no time for Ping-Pong
in these heady days.

He settled
on the wrong mania!
grumbles my friend.
I was just
getting good.

I study his face
and, beyond him,
Yukiko's back.
I've lost my appetite
for political action
and Yen Yi, but I know
the work they do
is good and for the sake
of us all. To pine
for Ping-Pong
over that? I remember
Sow Fong's denial, his smirk,

his indifference to the history
of our oppression
in this land, remind myself he's not
a lifelong friend, raised up
with me in the village.
That I've known him
mere months.

I ask him why he joined
the Resistance. Was it
for the Ping-Pong lessons
from Yen Yi?

No, no! he says. *The Ping-Pong
came first. That's
how he decided
somehow
that I was to be trusted, that I
was one of "them."*

Was he afraid to say no
to being recruited, for fear
of losing
the Ping-Pong lessons?

*The Ping-Pong
was great, but I was happy
to connect with Yen Yi
any way I could. I'd still
be in the Resistance except
it's no longer a way to get
anywhere near the guy.*

I admit to him
that Yen Yi has
a certain magnetism.

Yen Yi,
he informs me
with that smirk of his,
is an overbearing
bore.

surrounded

I'm surrounded by mysteries
I have no more desire
to plumb:

Sow Fong's
impenetrable brain.

What to think
about the Resistance,
the Association,
Yen Yi.

What became
of my letter
to Yukiko.

I avoid
Boocher's eyes
at meals, not wanting
to see yet again
his apologetic shrug
when I raise
a hopeful look.

He seems
to avoid me, too,
no longer pestering me
for details about
the noble and victorious
Resistance (which
is just as well, as I
have nothing to say about it
anymore), perhaps
as bummed as I am
that he only ever has
the bad news to give to me
of no news
about my letter.

And so
I jab the awl.

I throw myself
into my paper story studies
with a vehemence
that actually impresses Father.
I come to know our story so well, I start
to dream it. I think
of new questions we might be asked,
which are then smuggled out
to Thomas Lee in San Francisco
(by, yes, the Association
and therefore in part by Yen Yi),
the answers
smuggled back in to the kitchen and then
to the Association table and then
to us.

I will survive
interrogation. I will gain
the lower slopes
of Gold Mountain. I will labor
long and hard
for our benefactor, Thomas Lee.
I will follow Father's rules
for saving pennies here and earning
extra pennies there.

I will leave
Yen Yi, Sow Fong,
Yukiko behind
on this island they call Angel and find
in my new country
a house,
a job,
a girl,
a life.

ah

I'm sitting at dinner with Father,
who's talking about how
the banks in this country
will pay you interest
on the money
you store with them.

Grandfather
is at the next table over
with his Resistance committee,
gesturing with his hands
like he's as young
as the men he sits with.

Sow Fong is sitting
with me and Father. I've refrained
from asking him for any further clues
about his puzzling attitudes
toward anything. His third examination
is coming up, and we study together
in the far left corner of the rec yard,
quizzing each other
and inventing imaginary connections
between his paper people
and mine.

What if
your "sister"
is classmates
with my "brother's"
best friend?

What if
your "uncle"
is having a secret affair
with my "sister's"
best friend's
mother?

He's stifling a yawn
at talk by my father
about stocks and bonds
when a roar goes up
that jolts me
to my feet.

Another riot!

But no, it's only
in one corner of the hall,
a limited commotion
drawing all eyes.

A fight?

It's over
in a second. Father
nods his head
as the instant mob

disperses, mutters
that it's nothing,
sits.

The crowd
clears some more, men
resume their seats
and their meals, and then
I see: Boocher
bloodied and slumped
in a corner.

Ah, says Sow Fong. *It's just
the Black ghost spy.*

too many eyes

Dinner continues. Boocher
wobbles to his feet.
The kitchen manager yells
for him to clear
that table.

I scan the crowd for signs
of Boocher's opponent. I see
disheveled hair or clothing
on a few (Yen Yi,
for one), as if
they had tried
to intervene, perhaps
break up the fight,
but no one
with any real damage.

I want to run over
to Boocher, make sure
he's okay. Ask him
what the hell
just happened.

Sit! my father
hisses.

Newbie . . .
Teegee, says Sow Fong.

I sit.

Boocher
carries a load
back to the kitchen.
The guards still stand
by the door, as if
they'd made no move
to stop the fight
or apprehend
the fighters.

Mealtime
ends. We return
to the barracks—
where cheers go up
the moment the guards
shut the door. Where Yen Yi
is mobbed by a crowd
shaking his hand and clapping him
on the back.

He rises
to speak.

Thank you.
Thank you all, but it wasn't
just me. It was a band of us
who took the risk, who did
what needed to be done.

Is this about
what happened with Boocher
in the dining hall? Was it more
than a simple fight? Whatever
it was, Yen Yi
is taking bows for it.

He recites
a list of names.
The men step forward
or raise a hand, to cheers,
and then I understand:
four men ganged up
on one young guy
about my age.

With, of course,
the blessing—the mandate,
even—of my comrades
in the Association.

More cheers.

For those
who are unaware: today
we taught a lesson, a lesson
in consequences, to all
who would seek
to attack us, whether
through the use
of hostile examiners,
instigating guards,
or spies.

I look for Grandfather,
who is now a member
of Yen Yi's apparatus.
Did his committee
discuss this action? Did they

approve it, passing it up
the chain of command
until it reached
the Association table?

I spot Sow Fong
on a bunk, his head
bent over
a paper story cheat sheet.

Father
is conferring with a group
of cronies. They're frowning
but nodding,
as if making and agreeing with
important points
about the virtues
that outweigh the flaws
of Yen Yi
and the Association.

I try to catch
Yen Yi's attention, but there
are too many eyes,
throughout the room,
seeking his.

occasionally

Ten meals go by, all
with Boocher still
on the job. I sit
in my old place
in one corner of the hall,
the place we used to talk,
but he comes near only
to wordlessly
set down dishes.

I can't say
I blame him. I'm sure
he's mad at me for what
my people, my Resistance,
did to him. I want to tell him
that I'm sorry, that it wasn't me
or anything I wanted
or approved of, but I'm
bizarrely mad as well.

Mad at myself
for not defending him
more strongly
to Yen Yi, both before
and after the attack.

Mad at Boocher
for making me so
pathetically mad
at myself.

Mad at myself again
for making it all
about me when it was he
who was beaten up.

Ten meals go by as we each
stew in our anger, mine
with a side of guilt, the only change
from day to day, from meal
to meal, his slowly
healing wounds.

Grandfather tells me only
that he's no longer involved
in any committees.
He spends his hours
as before: moving along
and up and down
the walls, squinting
at the testimony
of the past
and present.

Sow Fong and I
continue studying our paper stories
in the far left corner of the rec yard.
It's my fifth month

in detention, and I have yet
to be questioned once.

Yukiko occasionally looks over
but always with the same
expression. *What's with her?*
blurts Sow Fong. *If she's not
going to write back, why
does she keep waving?*

I begin to wonder
if she actually has
written back, if Boocher,
in his anger, is refusing
to deliver her reply.
I curse him, curse myself
for stooping to a new
pathetic low: I'm now
mad at myself for being mad
at Boocher for entirely
imagined reasons.

two minutes

I'm sitting in my corner seat
in the dining hall, lonely
in the throng.

Sow Fong
never joins me here.
(I'm not cut out
to be a spy.) He's out there
somewhere, probably telling
a funny story or rehearsing
his own paper tale.

Father is probably
swapping proverbs
and assertions with his crew.
Grandfather, no longer
on a committee, is probably just
masticating, as alone
as I am, though he seems
to need only a bowl of rice
or a poem on the wall
for company.

Occasionally,
I glance

toward Yen Yi
at the Association
table.

Boocher comes over
with a dish of rice,
and I don't try
to meet his eyes.

He doesn't move.

I take a few bites. I focus
on my food. He goes on
standing there like
my personal guard
or servant.

Do I need to clear
some obstacle from the table
so he can set
the damn rice down?

When I finally
look up, he begins
to set down the rice
but slowly, passing it
close to my face so that
I see, pinned
by his hand to the bottom
of the dish, a sheet
of folded paper.

I realize
what it must be
and look up at him
with wild glee, but his face
is tight-lipped, even
grim, and I
take the cue.

I wait
a full two minutes
before
retrieving the note.

my own

Dear Yip Jing,

I'm glad
we can finally do more
than stare at each other
through a fence. We heard
about the riot
at your meal, and afterward
the yard stood empty day
after day, though
we did see lights
and movement
in your windows. Then
we heard how it all
came out.

We owe you thanks, because
our food and our conditions
have improved as well,
though they were probably
better than yours
to begin with.

I hear that you
were one of the rioters. How

did you find the strength? What
did it feel like? I dream
of action, but it's always set
in some world
not my own.

Is there writing
on the walls
of your barracks?
The walls of our rooms,
every inch, are covered
with poems!

There are poems
where poems have already
been written and faded
with the years, poems beneath
the already old paint
on the walls. They speak
of the hopes, the struggles,
and sometimes
the despair of those
who came before us.

They made me want to write
my own, for the first time
since leaving home. Here's
the first one I wrote
in our new country:

> *Falling petals,*
> *poems inscribed on the walls*
> *of my heart.*

old times

I'm electrified,
on fire, the morning light
that streams
into the barracks through
barred windows. I'm lit
with hope, desire, with
gratitude to the universe,
Yukiko, Boocher.

Boocher, my friend,
who undertook for me, whom I
suspected and failed
to console or stand up for
after his beating
by my people.

I spot Yen Yi
excusing himself
from a circle
of admirers. I follow him
to the upstairs lavatory,
take a seat
right next to his
in the otherwise
empty room.

Just
like old times,
eh, kid?

I tell him Boocher
is no spy. I tell him
why I'm sure: *He knows*
about the cheat notes
that are smuggled in.
He knows and hasn't told. If
he were their spy, they'd know
about them too.

Hmmm. Yen Yi nods. *Maybe*
you're right. Maybe he's not
a spy. Maybe he is. But if
he's not, it doesn't mean
he can be trusted. If he is,
it doesn't mean he might not also
keep some secrets
from his employers. With spies,
you don't get loyalty,
you only get
what you pay for.

So that's
why you beat him up?
I retort. *Because of*
"maybe, maybe not"?

Listen,
kid. What's really
bugging you? Your belief

that Boocher isn't a spy or that
we should not
have used force? If you were sure
that somebody *is a spy, that* somebody
is working intently
and through deceit
to send you and your family back
to China, to keep
all Chinese from entering
this country, no matter how desperate
their plight back home—a plight
made worse
by the aggressions
of the Western powers—no matter
how much skill or knowledge
or labor they might have
to offer this raw land,
would you then be okay
with giving him
a beating?

I find
no answer
to make.

No one who holds power
has ever given it up
without a fight.

No one
who holds power would hesitate
for a moment
to use it

to keep
what they have.

If Boocher was not
the spy, then
someone else was.
And he
saw what happened
to the one
we thought it was.

my dragon

Ten minutes later, still drunk
from the wine
of Yukiko's letter (spiked
with Yen Yi's rhetoric
of force and aggression),
I'm playing another game of Go
with Grandfather, this time
on even terms, refusing
my usual six stones
of help. Sick
of always defending
against his incursions and lured
by the strange blank slate
of an empty opening board,
I attack his stones
with abandon, refusing to cede
a single point of ground until—
I don't get even now
how it happened—his groups
are suddenly all quite safe, and I
am the one on the run.

My enormous dragon
of a group—half my stones
on the board afloat

without a base—writhes
and twines but is cut off
again and again
from any escape, devours stones
of Grandfather's only to find
the life it thought to gain
to be false, flies headlong
into a wall that might
as well have been
a literal
wall of stone.

It's the most titanic battle
we've had—and then
I'm staring (and
trembling? Am
I trembling?) at the truth
of the board: my dragon
is dead.

I get up in disgust, though this
is the result I should have
more than expected
without my usual
six-stone advantage.

I begin
to walk away.

Grandson!
Come back!

Grandfather bangs a stone
repeatedly on the board
like an impatient rich man
ringing for a servant.

We have to talk
about this game!

But there are letters
to be written, too many other talks
to be had. I am reminded,
though, of the courtesies.

Good game, I call back
over my shoulder as I
go out the door.

better

Sorry! I'm telling Boocher
over and over. *I'm sorry. I'm*
so sorry. I should have
stood up for you more
with the Resistance. But
I've told them now. I told them
how I know
you're not a spy.

Do you think
it will do any good?
he asks.

I have to say
no. He smiles.

That's the spirit, he says
without a trace
of irony. *Do the right thing,*
no matter what
the results, no matter
how it might turn
to your own disadvantage.

Sometimes I
forget that too.

He looks
grimly at me.
I imagine the wealth
of hard experience
behind his words. I form
an unexpected resolve.

I reach
into my pocket. Pull out
my next letter to Yukiko.

Look, I say. *I appreciate*
your delivering
the first one. Let's find
someone safer
for the rest. I know
you'd get in bigger trouble
if you were caught.

He stares at me
with an expression
I can't interpret. Is it
mockery, disbelief,
or wonder? He finally
laughs.

Naw, he says.
I'll do it. It's best
for me to do it. To find
a new person, for him

to find the way: that
would be the risk. And . . .
you can trust me.
To deliver. Better
the devil you know,
right?

reach

Dear Yukiko,

There are poems
here, too. My grandfather
reads them over and over,
all day long. I
read them too.

So you can read
and write? None
of the girls in my village
can do either.

Your poem
is beautiful, and different.
It doesn't rhyme or scan,
but I really like
how short and simple it is. How
you put into words
the way the poems on our walls
make me feel, how you put
those words into a poem
of your own.

I tried
to write a poem
on our walls but was busted
by the Association.
Do they have any reach
into your quarters?
They pretty much rule
in ours. They actually
put me in a jail
within our jail, a room
they stick you in, but I wrote
a poem there! If I can sneak
back in there, and if
they haven't found it
and erased it, I'll copy it
and send it to you.

The riot came
from nowhere. It caught
almost everybody
by surprise, and I
had to decide in a second
whether I would be in it.
I'm glad
I made the choice I did,
but I don't agree with everything
the leaders of what we call
the Resistance do.

windows

Dear Yip Jing,

My father is a scholar
literate in Japanese,
Chinese, and English.
He taught me and my mother
to read and write
in all of them. He's Japanese
but met my mother on a trip
to our city, and we lived there
through my childhood.

It wasn't
easy.

I'm only
on the Chinese side of detention
because I'm with
my mother. If my father
were with us, we'd probably
already be landed. He waits for us
in San Francisco, in a district
where we'll live
with other Japanese.

I don't know
if that
will be easier.

I'm glad
you liked my poem.
Here's one
I wrote last night:

Just as bright
on this side of the sky, the moon
through barred windows.

whose ending

Do I tell her
the story—whose ending
I don't even know—
of the Japanese man
who once lived
in our village?
I tell her instead
about the seven-foot man,
how his persecution
by the pale powers—but also
his loneliness
among us, our failure
to surmount the high walls
of his isolation—brought him
to the end
of that rope, swinging
like a pendulum
outside the shut door
of our prison.

I copy his poem
into my letter, Grandfather
looking over my shoulder
as I squat
at the base of the wall.

That's a poem
worth remembering,
he tells me.

I go on
to tell her how the death
of the seven-foot man
led to our action that led
to change. I tell her
about Yen Yi.

I can't deny
he's brave and cares
about our people, or that
he and the Association
have done a lot of good, but I can't
follow him anymore, especially
after he and his gang
beat up Boocher . . .

Here,
I must again spell out a name
in English letters, no other way
to communicate a string
of sounds. But will she
recognize them as the name
of the person I mean?

. . . the guy
who delivers
these letters to you.

Then I tell her
the news we learned
just yesterday.

My first examination
comes in two weeks. Have you
been questioned yet?

Maybe
we'll both be landed
around the same time.
I think we have a lot
in common. We can both
read and write in more
than one language.
We both come out
to the places where
we see each other, you
on your bench, me
in this corner
of our rec yard, to get away
from the suffocating air
of our dorms.

I will also
be living in San Francisco. We
should stay in touch.

so many more

I dream that night
of Yukiko dreaming
of action. She sits, her back
to me, with the guard
beside her, at a desk
cluttered with flower petals
that are papers with poems
written on them. When she turns
to wave hello to me, her face
is the face of my sister.

I spend the day
revisiting old theories
about who rescued me
the day
I almost drowned.

My number one suspect
has always been
Grandfather.

Who else knew
what we did
at the river? Who else
would haul me back

to my own bed?
Who else would keep
the secret
of my disobedience?

Yet he's not
so strong. He might
have drowned
himself. He could barely
walk all the way out
to the river, much less
drag my body back.

Could it have been
Kow Loon?

I picture her spending
her strength beside me
in the fields—for what?
A house? A job?
To be the girl
of someone else's
life?

I picture her
beside me, learning
the new world's
tongue.

I picture her tailing me
on one of my secret trips
to the river, watching me
and my friends

make the crossing, stand
victorious on the rocks
of the far side, wishing
she could be
one of us.

Did she
tail me out
to the river
that day?

I never understood
why she wanted to learn
to read and write. Then I realized
she might have the same desires
for her children that
our mother did. Now I wonder
if she's picturing me
this moment, wishing
she could have tailed me
on this journey I would not
wish upon
my worst enemy, that *she*
could be here, not just
for the future generations
but for herself.

At dinner, I look
across the rows of tables, counting
all the stories packed
into this crowded hall. Knowing
that for every man
who thinks himself

the only hero of the story
of his family, there are wives
and daughters, sisters
and mothers, left
back home or waiting
like us, across the way
in the women's dorm,
whose stories still wait
to be told.

only the light

Dear Yip Jing,

John Brown
was beaten up
by a gang of those
who lead your Resistance?

I didn't know. He
didn't tell me.

What
strange creatures
we are, that harm
our own kind.

My mother and I
have been questioned once
so far, at the same time
but separately, I suppose
so we couldn't
compare answers. But who
would want to repeat
some of the questions
we were asked, questions that if
a man were to ask them of me

on the street, he'd be arrested
for indecency?

Good luck
with your examination. Here's
a poem I wrote for you, for when
the moment comes:

> *Is that the face of a god*
> *among the clouds? Only the light*
> *of what will be.*

Dear Yukiko,

Is John Brown
the name of the guy
who delivers these letters
to you? We know him
as Boocher.

They beat him up
because they thought
he was a spy—they still
think he is—but I
know he's not. Someday,
I'll tell you how
I know.

It's sad
how we suspect one another, though
in the case of our interrogators,
we have good reason. I've heard
how even those with a right to land
can be turned away by failing questions
about their homes or villages
that no one

would ordinarily know
the answers to.

Thank you
for your poem. I liked it
and will remember it
in my hour
of trial.

the plan

In truth, I don't
understand her poem or even
how it's encouraging.

What if "what will be"
is that I'm rejected?
Who wouldn't want
a god in the clouds
to aid him? But of course,
you can't say such things.

We go on
exchanging letters
almost every day. I continue
to study my paper story. Conditions
continue to improve, the work
of Yen Yi
and the Association.
Burned-out lights
are fixed. The sink
we do our laundry in—
never designed
for such a use, but how else
would we wash our things?—

is replaced by a bigger one
with a greater flow.

I get a letter from Yukiko
that begins, *You shouldn't*
call him Boocher. His name
is John Brown. But every time
I call to him, I can't get
"John Brown"
out of my mouth—it sounds
so arbitrary, like a pair
of nonsense syllables, and everybody
calls him Boocher, and he doesn't
seem to mind.

Yip Jing! he says
to me one morning. *We have*
a problem. They're taking me off
the women's meal shifts, but
we have a plan. Yukiko
will find a way to leave her letters
by the fence where she sees you
in the afternoons, and
to pick up any letters
you leave there. She'll leave them
under a rock or bush,
so look around.

I thank him
for the news, the help,
the plan
that preserves a path
to the future.

Now you,
he adds, *can do* me
a favor: Will you
deliver this
to her?

Of course, I say,
taking the folded sheets
he holds out to me
while thinking,
What the hell?

what

I scrutinize
Boocher's face, hiding
my own surprise. He
wants to send her letters
too? Has he
already been? His face
betrays
no answers.

Boocher! shouts
the kitchen boss.

Sow Fong's face
furrows in disgust
when I ask him
what he makes
of this.

Okay, he finally
replies. *Okay.*
First thing: he can't
be into her. Okay?
He can't. Because
he knows you are,
right? If he knew

you were, why
would he have agreed
to carry your letters?
Why wouldn't
he have told you no,
it can't be done?

I think about how
at first, he told me
exactly that.

And because—
well, damn it:
because!

His arms
flail outward,
as if trying
to embrace
a mountain.

Hey, he brightens,
the letter! His letter.
We can steam it open—
hell, rip it open, stick it
in a new envelope,
who would know
the difference?—find out
what he's up to.

I pull the folded,
unsecured sheets
from my pocket.

What?
laughs Sow Fong. *Well,*
whether he's after her
or not, the guy's
a fool.

I hold
Boocher's letter, all
the answers I need
within
my grasp.

Come on!
prods my friend. *What*
are you waiting for?

I take

By lights-out
(an hour later
than it used to be,
courtesy
of the Association's
new persistent voice
in the ears
of the pale powers) I still
haven't read the letter.
I set it, throughout the day,
on a bunk or table
or the ground
in front of me. Each time,
it slowly unfolds,
as if begging
to be read.

Whenever
I encounter Sow Fong,
he raises a brow, takes in
my silent reply,
and laughs as if I
am the fool. We sit
through the afternoon
in the far left corner

of the rec yard,
watching Yukiko
on her bench, seeking
a sign.

I nod
in affirmation
twice, to Boocher's
nod of thanks at lunch
and his look
of silent query
at dinner.

In my bed,
I dream of the moon
through barred windows
transforming
into a face, a breast,
the skin of a girl
I've never touched.

I wake
to darkness,
with the hard-on
of all hard-ons
crying out to me
for release.

I lower myself
to the floor, past
my sleeping father,
wheezing grandfather.
The lights in the lavatories

are usually left on for those
who need to use them
in the night.

I take
the letter with me.

an ardor

Your dreams of us
Are dreams I share.
I only say:
Beware!

Dreams are fleeting;
Life is long.
The end is clear,
But paths go wrong.

I dream a future
Free from harm.
I dream an ardor
In your arms.

But first we work
The daylit hours.
At night we dream
The moon through bars.

a plan

In addition
to the poem, there's a letter,
three pages long, addressing Yukiko as
"My dearest Yuki," detailing
the minutiae
of the hours he spent, both here
and in his Oakland home,
since (I suppose) the last time
he wrote her, raving
about a new young poet,
Langston Hughes, and ending
"Your John Brown."

Sow Fong
is furious,
militant. He won't
keep his voice down
at breakfast. *Fry*
the fucker! Fuck
the bastard! Boocher
passes close to us. I worry
Sow Fong will jump him
then and there. *I say*
we bust him up.
Yen Yi will help. No one

will say a word! You saw
what happened
before. They'll fucking
cheer us.

No, I tell him.

Why not? he cries.

I'm just as mad
as he is. More. I thought
of Boocher as a friend.
I trusted him. He told me
he could be trusted. I recall
how he tried at first
to tell me it couldn't be done,
till I threatened to find
a better messenger, and realize
I should have suspected him
from the start. I think
of Yen Yi's words, that even
if he isn't a spy, *it doesn't*
mean he can be trusted. Of what
Boocher said himself,
that *boss or worker, friend*
or foe, can both help you
and betray you. But I shrink
from the idea of violence. It feels
like a line I mustn't cross
or I'll be lost. I think
of the cheers received
by Yen Yi and his gang

for beating up Boocher,
and shiver.

We could rough him up,
I tell Sow Fong, *but what*
will she *think*
once she hears?

That
settles him down.

Okay. But
we have to do
something.

Ten seconds later,
he snaps his fingers:
Here it is! He likes her;
there's nothing you can do
about that. And she
likes him. *There's nothing*
you can say about that
without looking
like a jerk. Here's
the real problem: that he
got the jump on you,
that he was here
for who knows how long,
passing notes with her
before you even arrived. Who knows
what would have happened
if you had been here
from the start?

Now, what if
he got fired? He'd still
like her, sure, but he'd
be gone, out
of the picture, for as long
as she—and you—are here,
together. You'd get your chance
to make up ground.

We watch Boocher
on his rounds, being turned away
from the Association table, ordered
to move his lazy ass
by the kitchen boss. Writing
in his notebook. I ponder
whether an attack like this
would not still be
an act of violence.

Sow Fong proposes
a plan.

not one

Do I still
think Boocher's
a spy? Why
do you even say,
"still"?

Yen Yi leans back
in his chair. Around us
echo the grunts
of the Ping-Pong players,
their spectators' shouts,
the *Chī!* and *Pèng!*
of the mah-jongg players,
and the stone-fall
of their tiles.

Okay, then. Point
number one: of course
they're spying on us.
Why wouldn't they? They know
we're telling paper stories.
They'd be delinquent
if they didn't do
everything they could
to expose them. It's only

what we'd do ourselves
if our positions
were reversed.

He speaks more loudly
than he needs to just
to be heard by me above
the game room buzz.
The Ping-Pong players
suspend their game.
The mah-jongg tiles
go quiet. He's turning this
into a general lecture,
but that's fine by me.
I came for his help
and will take the help
of anyone else in the group.

Point number two: even
if every man here
was who he says he is,
they'd still be on the hunt
for reasons to turn us away.
Their talk of legal
or illegal is just a cover
for their true intentions,
a way to hate
by technicality.

The calls
of "Yes" and "Right"
from our audience

firm the shaky ground
I walked in on.

Finally, point
number three: you might
wonder why, if
they needed a spy, they'd use
a kid who's not
one of them. I say:
that's exactly
who they'd use. That's how
they work: to set us
against one another. Who else
would need as much
to curry their favor?
I'm sure the kid has problems
of his own, but that
is exactly why he's not
going to give a damn
about ours.

He turns
to look me
in the eyes.

I nod.

Yip Jing, you
know him best.
Have you seen any sign
he cares a whit
for us, or that he wouldn't
sell us out in a second

to gain an advantage
for himself?

I raise
my own voice
so it can be heard
by all: *Not*
one!

both bills

That afternoon,
I find Yukiko's first letter to me
delivered in the new way:
under a bush
conveniently abutting
the fence of the rec yard.
Sow Fong and I assume
she left it there while we
were at lunch, while
the rec yard was empty
and she could approach it
without raising the concern
of her guard. And therefore
that she won't be free to check
for anything left in the area
until the same time
the following day.

She's not there now, perhaps
to give us a chance
to pick up her letter
without her guard
close by.

We pool our cash
to acquire a pair of dollar bills,
then toss them outside the fence
with Boocher's letter
a few feet away.

Sow Fong
approaches a guard, points
to the bills outside the fence,
pantomimes them blowing
out of his hand and him
giving one to the guard
if he'll retrieve them both.

The guard finds the bills,
the letter. *What's that?*
asks Sow Fong in Chinese
the guard can't understand
but in a clearly puzzled tone,
craning his neck to see. (I marvel
at this final theatrical touch
we didn't plan.) *Is that*
English writing?

The guard returns both bills
and shoos Sow Fong, shuffles
the pages of the letter,
draws it closer to his face,
stands suddenly straight,
and rushes back
into the barracks and out
the door.

We track him through
a dormitory window all the way
into the administration building,
wait.

the touch

I wait
until I'm in my bunk
at the end of the day
to read Yukiko's latest.

Nothing happened
at dinner. Boocher
was still there. He looked
a piercing question at me;
a panicked nod
was all I could manage
in reply. He later came close
with a dish on his way
to another table,
and briefly laid his hand
on my shoulder.

Dear Yip Jing,

You can absolutely
trust John Brown. I
would trust him
with my life. I haven't
trusted easily. We've been despised
by the Chinese

all my life, even my mother,
who is Chinese but married
a Japanese man. No one
would talk to her at home.
No one will talk
to her here. It's easy
to believe the whole world
is against us, but my father
loved a woman who was not
of his own kind, and she
loved him though she knew
what that would mean
for herself. For each of them,
there was the one exception
to the rule, and if
there was one, then
why not others?

John Brown
is also despised
by everyone
in his world, except
his father and the poets
he loves. By those lights,
he saw me—my
heart—and became
one of my
exceptions.

Which
you are too, because
you wrote to me despite
what you must have been told

about me, what
you must have been taught
to think
about me.

In darkest night,
the uncountable stars
like so many friends.

All night, I feel
the touch
of Boocher's hand.

so close

Breakfast is another
normal meal: Boocher
serving tables, the Association
with a great bowl of congee
from which the smell
of roast duck wafts.
I sit with Sow Fong, not
in Boocher's corner,
but near the entrance
and its guards, a spot
where Boocher is unlikely
to stop and try
to speak with me.

I wonder
if our action
will have an effect
and if so, how and when
it will go down. I wonder
if I can even now
prevent it from occurring.
I tell myself that this
is what must be,
that I'm doing Yukiko a favor

by obstructing a relationship
that would only make her more
of a pariah.

That Boocher
might well
be a spy.

Hey, I start
to say to Sow Fong,
when two guards
appear at the door,
a man in a suit
at their head.
He points out Boocher,
and they advance,
surround him, and then
they're walking him
toward the door.

But, sir, he's saying,
I don't know what you mean
about a letter. If I
could just clear off
that table first. The boss
will be upset.

He's eyeing me
the whole time, as if
he knows. I lower my gaze
as he comes near me—
and am pushed

from the side, sent
careening
to the floor, a body
landing on top of me, the clang
of metal and shouts
and then—

The guards
are dragging Boocher
off me. Men are up
and in his face,
shouting, *What the hell?* and *What
did they do to* you?, and then,
as Boocher is led
out the door, they help
Sow Fong and me
to our feet, and Sow Fong
is shouting theatrically
to the hall, *What the fuck
was that? Did you see
what he did?* but later
whispers to me, *This
is perfect! If the letter alone
was not enough
to get him canned,
what he just did
is sure to do it.*

But I
can only think
of what happened
at the bottom of the scrum,
of Boocher's face

so close to mine, they nearly
touched. Of what
he said and what
he gave me, hidden
in my pocket.

IV. RELEASE

There are tens of thousands of poems composed on these walls.
They are all cries of complaint and sadness.
The day I am rid of this prison and attain success,
I must remember that this chapter once existed.

—Recovered from the walls of the men's barracks,
Angel Island Immigration Station

best light

I claim
to be woozy
from the blow,
get permission
to return
to the barracks.

Sow Fong walks me
to the dining hall door.

We did it!
I can't believe
it worked so well,
but how did he know
it was us? I thought
he was going to kill you!
Did you hear me
playing innocent? Hey,
are you seriously
not okay? Do you want me
to come along?

I wave him off.
A guard escorts me back
to the barracks and leaves.

I'm alone
in the forest
of bunks.

I have a half hour
before they all return.

I find
the best light. Pull
from my pocket
Boocher's notebook.

Begin to read.

you find

How do you come
to the end of your rope?

You start
with abject fear,
when you realize
that Boocher is the one
who slammed you
to the floor, that he's now
on top of you, his face
so close to yours,
he could bite your nose off
if he hated you
enough.

Then you see
he's grinning.
He winks. (Of course
he doesn't know! How
could he know?) His hands
are urging something
into yours. He says,
For her.

And then
you're reading
what he wrote: not
spy reports but thoughts
on life and friendship and, yes,
on love.

And poems.

You find poems
about America (*A land
of freedom / To enslave*),
some about war (*The dust
of those / Who won't
return*), and some
you don't understand:

They build a house
Of gilded cards.
Like piggies' houses,
It will fall.

Though mostly air,
Its fall will kill.
Their only instinct:
Higher still.

You find
a stanza that seems
to be about you.

A guy afloat,
About my years,

Not yet grown into
Tribal fears.

You find poems
and fragments about
and to Yukiko, including,
on the second to last
written page, the poem
you failed to deliver.

You find,
on the last
written page, a poem
that leaves you
swinging
like a pendulum
outside
the shut doors of
your prison.

a damn

I know
what I have to do.
I know
how little time
I have to do it.
I don't
know where
to begin.

And so I go
to Yen Yi.

You want to talk
to the Administration? Sure,
I could get you in, but they don't
really need your testimony. They
saw what happened as clearly
as we all did.

No time to finesse
the outcome I need.
I tell Yen Yi
what I did to Boocher.
He takes a step back,

looks me
up and down.

Comrade! I
salute you. I have
to say: I thought
you had quit
on us. But that
was a hero move.
I still don't see
why you need to talk
to the Administration.

I find it hard
to name the thing
I already decided
to do, as if
I haven't fully decided
until I say out loud,
To confess. Then
I know
I'm going to do it.

Wait, what? What
are you thinking?

I tell him
I can't let Boocher
be fired because of something
I did.

Okay, replies Yen Yi,
calming the air

with his hands,
first off, you're not
going to save him.
That he hoped you wouldn't
leak his letter does not
excuse him writing it. That
you leaked the letter
does not excuse him
jumping you.

You're not
going to save him—
never mind why
you even want to (I don't
want to hear it!)—
so what remains? Your
honest soul? If that's
the case, will you also
confess your real name
while you're at it, disavow
your paper story?

I'm left,
as usual,
without a word to say
in the wake
of Yen Yi's logic.

We owe
no truth to men
who will consign us
to despair
if we can't remember

the number of dishes
in the cupboard
of our childhood home.
I don't give a damn
about our jailers
or their spy, but you
I care about.
Do what you plan,
and you'll only
get yourself
rejected.

the shapes

I thought
I knew what I have
to do. I still
need to do
something but know
I can no longer do
what I planned.

How many more
of my certainties
will crumble? What's left
of what has to
be done?

I dream of action,
but it's always set
in some world not
my own.

I wander
into the game room.
Grandfather
is sitting at the Go board,
alone, hunched

over a pattern
of stones.

Grandson!
Another game?

I shake my head
but smile. There's comfort
in the small world
of his passions.

Grandfather,
I laugh, *you wiped me out*
last time!

He smiles, rises,
gestures for me
to sit. Calls me
by my real name.

He's smiling
still, so I can only guess
he forgot the proper
security precautions, but I find
I can't ignore the invocation
of my true
and hidden self.

I sit.

He clears the board but moves
both bowls of stones
to his side

of the table and then proceeds
to play the moves
for both sides in silence
broken only
by the click, click, click
of stones snapped down
onto the board without
a moment's pause.

It takes me a while to see
he's replaying
our last game.

He pauses
at the point he tried
to surround a group of mine
on the side of the board
and instead of defending it,
I turned around
to attack
his attackers.

Here, he says,
*is where my heart
began to sing.*

No kidding,
I think, but he goes on
to say, *In every game
we played before, here
is where you would cower,
when you would retreat to safety
and let me surround you.*

But why? Your group
is stronger than mine.
You have more stones
in the area. You should—
and finally did!—
attack.

Except, I want to retort,
that my attack
got smashed, and I think
not just of our game
but of my attack on Boocher
and how it, too, ended
in disaster. But Grandfather
continues playing moves
and talking.

Here
was your first mistake.
My group was strong now, but you
continued to attack.
And this group of mine
was already connected
to its fellows and therefore
unassailable. Meanwhile,
your own attackers
were never connected, never
had a base. You see it
here? And here?

I do. Or do
begin to. We've never
done this, analyzed

a game we played. Unburdened
by the imperatives of battle,
I begin to see the board
as a whole.

You must attack
wherever your opponents
are weak. If you don't,
you grant them
unearned profit. That
was the lesson
you learned and why
our last game
was the best
you've ever played.

The next lesson
is this: you must attack
from strength.

As if
the board were shaken
and all the stones
resettled into their exact
previous positions
but somehow different, I see,
for the first time, the shapes
of my stones.

only

I know now
what I truly
have to do but have
no better idea
how to do it. I go,
this time,
to Sow Fong.

You want
to WHAT? He peers at me
suspiciously. *Why*
would you want
to do that?

I have no choice
but to tell him all
that I now desire, so much more
outrageous than my original
desire that my words
grow weaker
and more stilted
as I speak.

So, anyway,
that's it, I finish.

It's what—I know it
now—I have to do.

Sow Fong stares at me
so blankly,
so intently,
and for so long, I worry
he didn't hear
what I said, or worse:
he's preparing
the mocking,
scathing rejoinder
of his life.

Okay,
he finally replies. *Your*
funeral. So what's
the plan?

Here
is where my heart
begins to sing, because
I see his face
is pinched with worry
or incomprehension, yet
he's going to help me do
what I have to do, only
because I said I have
to do it.

I
have no idea,

I laugh. *You're*
the schemer.

Okay, he says,
I'm on it, but then
his expression pinches
again. *You know*
no good
can come of this,
right? That he could use
this against you to divert
some blame from his own
damn self?

I reply
with a Go proverb
that Grandfather has uttered
at one point or another
in every game
we've ever played
but that I'm now
just beginning to hear: *only*
surrounded groups
can be killed.

the final thing

I peer
through a window toward
the administration building, probe
the fencing around the rec yard
looking for a spot
I might climb before the guards
can stop me. For all
I know, they might
already have shipped him
off the island, my redirected effort
might be too late, but all
I can do now
is try.

It occurs to me
I might not return
from this. I find Father
in the game room
with the group
around the Victrola.
I take the seat beside him, lean
into his shoulder
for a minute. He squirms
but remains
in his seat, allows me

to snuggle against him like
I haven't done since
maybe ever as the strange
Western music
washes over us.

I can remain only
a minute, but just
as I'm about to get up,
Sow Fong appears,
waving and smiling
at the door. He flashes
a quick thumbs-up. Is then
displaced by a guard
who scans the room, fixes
on me, and heads
my way.

I feel
like my plan—when
I don't even have one yet—
has been exposed
and they're coming
to bust me, but Sow Fong
was smiling, and now
he's back in the doorway,
smiling still. The guard
calls out my name.

Yip Jing Lee?
Yip Jing Lee!

Father
is on his feet, demanding
what the guard wants
and why but in Chinese
and there's no interpreter,
but I take another glance
at Sow Fong's smiling face
and tell my father, *It's all right.*
They want to ask me
about what happened
in the dining hall.

The guard leads me out
onto the grounds, not
to the administration building
but to a truck by the front gate,
where two guards are loading
a prisoner.

I can't believe
that Sow Fong
managed this. How
did Sow Fong
manage this?

We reach the car,
and my guard tells
the other two, *They said*
to let them talk
before you take that one
to the ferry.

I'm standing
face-to-face
with Boocher.

The guards are just
a few steps off. Maybe
they'll hear me,
maybe they won't.

I say
what I have to say.

I set you up.
I leaked your letter
to the guards.
I'm sorry. I did it
because I was jealous
of you and Yukiko.
I did it because—
I realize this
as I speak—*because*
you're not Chinese.

His face contorts
but with what?
Rage? Incredulity? Will he
attack me again? Shout
to the guards that I
should be put off
the island, sent
back home, like him?

He laughs.

Okay, man.
Okay! It actually
makes me feel
better.

About what?

I didn't deliver
your letter at first. I almost
never did. Same
reason, more or less.

I think back to Yukiko's
long silence even as
she continued to wave and smile
from her bench like nothing
was amiss. It all
makes sense now, except:

What made you
change your mind?

He looks me
up and down.

It's hard
to describe. It happened
after they jumped me.

After the Resistance
beat him up? How

does that make sense?
Then I see it
and I say it: *Because*
we have to stick
together?

He smiles
and raises to me,
once more, the salute
of that outward-facing fist.

I'll step aside,
I tell him. *You*
were first,
she's yours.

He frowns.

No one can own
another human being.
If anyone
will be her friend—
or lover—that's
for her to say.
You understand?

I nod
and tell him
the final thing
that's needed.

John Brown,
my real name
is Soo Tai Go.

Tai Go? he says.
Okay, Tai Go. Why don't
you look me up
when you get out?
My full *name is*
John Brown
Boucher.

completely different

I did see "Boucher"
written out
in his notebook but assumed
it was pronounced
like everybody has been saying it
all along. I still don't see
how those English letters
could make that sound,
but now I know
my ignorance
means nothing.

On the walk back
to the barracks, through tears—
I haven't cried
since I was six—every inch
of the grounds, every board
and brick of the buildings,
the sky itself look exactly
like they did before and yet
completely different, like the stones
on Grandfather's board, or glances
exchanged across a distance,
or the sound of a name

you thought
you knew.

I enter the barracks,
and Sow Fong comes running,
bouncing off bunks and bodies
like whitewater through rocks
that only agitate
its passage, a look
on his face that makes me wonder,
as he slams into me, if he's
been crying too.

He holds me until
I want to squirm
out of his grasp, until
I want to say
something smart and rude
to break the spell, and then
I don't. I think
of my moment
with John Brown, the test
I failed and failed
but finally passed. About how
I'll never be able to tell the story
to anyone who matters to me
except maybe Mother
on some
unimaginable day, how
Sow Fong is the only one
who knows what I did,
even if he thought
I was a fool

to try it, and I accept
the congratulations he's not
even offering.

When he finally lets go,
his usual smirk
is back on his face.

So you didn't get arrested
right on the spot,
he says, and I tell him,
No such luck.

Father appears,
and I assure him
all is well.

It was just
as I said, I tell him,
and he brightens.

This
could be good,
he says. *This*
could help us
with our entry,
that we cooperated
with their investigation.

Grandfather is next
and asks for every detail
of my fictitious interview
with the investigators.

I do my best to conjure
a kind of second
paper story.

Then
they asked me
if I have any idea
why he tackled me,
and I told them
no, that he and I
are friends.

It's another twenty minutes
before we're alone
and I can ask Sow Fong
how he pulled off
getting me that time
with John Brown.

It wasn't me,
he says. *But I'll take credit*
for knowing where to go
in a pinch. The one to thank
is Yen Yi.

a sense

Well, Yen Yi
is saying, *I'm glad*
you escaped
unscathed.
So far.

We're sitting
in the corner of the dining hall
where I used to talk
with John Brown. The food
is just coming out, and I wonder
if he'll hustle right back
to the Association table
once we're done.

I ask him
why he helped, when he first
tried to talk me out of
doing anything.

Your friend, he says,
persuaded me
that we should help you out
no matter how
stupidly selfish

and self-destructive
your mixed-up intentions
might be. And he
was right; he only
reminded me of what
I too often forget: that
not everybody
is as smart
as I am.

So, I venture, returning
his smile, *are you also persuaded*
that John Brown
was no spy?

Ha! he cries, a sound
between a laugh
and a martial arts
bellow. *What*
is your deal
with that guy?

Listen,
he continues.
Listen to me, because
I'm only
going to say this—hell,
who am I kidding?
I'm going to say this
over and over,
a thousand times
if I have to. Or better yet,

take a look
at this!

He pulls from his pocket
a dimpled triangular stone
with an odd texture,
like it's been chipped
down to edges
and a point.

I found this
on the grounds
my first week here,
he tells me. *I had no idea*
what it even was
until that reporter who came
to do the story on me
told me it was an arrowhead
made by the Miwok,
the people who lived here
first, whoe name
means literally
"The People."

Wherever they are, whatever
became of them, we
are now The People
on this island, the new
inconvenience
the Americans are trying
to be rid of.

You and I?
We're kin. No matter
who asks me for help,
no matter why, if
he's one of us, if he's of
The People, I'll give him
all I have.

If he's not?
If he's someone
not kin to me? Then I
don't owe him
a sneer.

You
got it?

I find a sense
in which I can agree
wholeheartedly. It all depends,
it always has and always will,
on whom you include
as kin. "Dark-skinned,"
"half-Chinese," "half-Japanese." Even
(I can see myself coming
to see someday) the "pale,"
however powerful
they might be. The labels
I once employed to organize
my world. We're all
The People.

I give Yen Yi
a *Got it!*
and a smile and
my hand.

Now
let's eat!
he says, clapping
his hands and looking
around the hall. *I'm*
ravenous. How long
does it take
for the food
to get all the way
back here?

the final poem

After lunch,
I go out
to the far left corner
of the rec yard. There's been
no time or privacy
to write a letter, so
I do it now, though there's still
no privacy, because
I couldn't shake
Sow Fong.

Yukiko,

I've made
a terrible mistake
that caused John Brown
to be fired.

Yukiko on her bench
glances over and smiles,
gesturing toward the bush
where she left her letter.
I nod and hold up
the paper I'm writing on
to let her know

I got her letter
and a reply
is on its way.

I'm so sorry
for how it turned out.
I did what I did
from my feelings
for you, though I realize
we hardly know each other
yet. Your letters
were so wonderful, and I
got jealous
of John Brown.
It caught me by surprise
that you and he
are close, but he's
forgiven me, as I hope
you will someday,
and I want you to know
that I will spend
the rest of my life . . .

I look up
from the letter
into the boundless blue
of the sky. How
will I spend
the rest of my life?

Newb! says
Sow Fong. *What*

have you written
so far?

I sigh
and read what I have
aloud to him.

Stop! Stop! Stop!
he's yelling before
I've read it all. *What*
are you thinking?

I have
no clue
what he's peeved about.
I already told him
what I was going to write and thought
he accepted it, however
grudgingly.

He plunges on
into my silence.

You were stupid
to like her
in the first place.
Stupider
to confess what we did
to Boocher.
Are you trying to set
a record?

I say, *But I have to*
apologize.

Fine! he shouts, so loudly
that I glance around the yard
to count how many eyes
he's drawn. *Then do it!*
Apologize. For real.
Don't try
to explain or excuse,
or worse: to lay
on her
the burden of forgiving
your sorry ass.

I want
to hit him.
Will he always
find fault? Can
he only insult
without
understanding?

Then I see,
once more,
the shape
of my stones.

I tear the paper,
begin
anew:

Yukiko,

I've done
a hateful thing.
I sabotaged
John Brown
in order to get him
fired. He wrote
a letter to you,
entrusted it
to me, and I
betrayed him,
handing it over
to a guard.

There's no excuse
for what I did,
no explanation
other than
evil intent. I'm sorry
for the harm
I caused you both.

I sign the letter
with my real name,
then add: *The second to last poem*
in this notebook, the one
John Brown carried around
and wrote in, was part
of the letter he wrote you. I think
he would have gone on
to send you
the final poem as well.

I write out
a copy
of that final poem
for myself, then fold my letter
into the notebook
and leave them
under the shrub.

you and me

black boy
stack crates
serve food
clear plates

"yes, sir"
"right away"
never say
"someday"

"slant eyes"
"yellow threat"
just people
at their bread

locked up
held down
penned in
kept out

fair face
black skin
two souls
within

you and me
both enslaved
by needless fear
by endless pain

who would send us

And now
all that remains
is to pass
our interrogations,
which I once thought
would be the climax
of my story but now
feels more
like an epilogue.

Sow Fong goes in
for his third, returns
upbeat: *I think*
we fooled them
good!

The Association deliver
a final study sheet
from Thomas Lee. My father
thanks them, bows, turns
to go read the letter. I
remain, facing
my former jailers. I once
thought they linked their hands
with those of the pale powers

to bar our way
to the lower slopes
of Gold Mountain. Now
I see them as fellow travelers,
hands linked with ours, taking
slow steps forward against
a howling wind.

I bow to them.

Thomas Lee writes
that he's been called in
to tell his side
of our story, but his appointment
is the same day
that Father and Grandfather and I
are scheduled ourselves,
so there won't be a chance
to send us a report
of the questions he's asked.

We go in
on a foggy, drippy morning
that makes me shiver,
that reminds me of the winters
in our village. They seat us
in a waiting room, call
Grandfather first, then
Father, as I sit thinking
of a thousand futures
that might be. And then
I'm called.

I enter a room
with an empty chair
in front of a table
where the examiner
and his interpreter sit.
There are guards in the room
but not the ones
who witnessed my final meeting
with John Brown,
come to tell
what they overheard
between us.

They ask me
my name, and my mind
goes blank
for just one second
before I reply.

Which direction
did our house face? What
were the names
of all the families
on our street? Who was
the oldest man
in our village? I'm amazed
that all these questions
have been covered
in our cheat sheets.

They ask me a question
that wasn't: Who
were all my teachers

year by year? But I realize
the answer must be
that Thomas Lee's village
was the same
as ours—*We didn't have*
a school—or it would have been
on a cheat sheet.

They ask more questions
I'm prepared for. They ask
another unaccounted
question: How many chairs
were in our house? I have to
fall back on *I can't*
remember.

When I tell them the house
had seven doorways, the examiner
looks suddenly up, and I think,
Oh, shit!

He asks me,
Are you sure?

I think back
through all the paper facts
I've learned, decide
that I am sure. It's seven. It's got
to be seven. Unless
the others
answered wrong.

I'm sure,
I say.

Your "grandfather"
said five. Your "uncle"
six. Are you
still sure?

They have us. Or are
they bluffing me?

I think
of Yen Yi's line
about men
who would send us away
for not remembering
the number of dishes
in the cupboards
of our childhood homes,
of the artifact
of a displaced people
he keeps
in his pocket.

I think
of Sow Fong's theatrics
when we leaked the letter
to the guard and in
the aftermath
of John Brown's takedown
in the dining hall. *(Did*
you hear me
playing innocent?)

I scowl.

My grandfather's, like,
a thousand years old,
and Uncle
hasn't been home
for years. Who
are you going to
believe?

I hold
my confident pose.
The interpreter
mimics
my indignant tone
with a touch
of comedic flair.
The examiner
chuckles,
moves on.

A dozen questions later,
I'm released into a room
where Father and Grandfather
wait with anxious looks
that I answer with a smile
and a nod. We return
to the barracks, where
we're grilled by the others
for every detail and discover
that Grandfather
got more answers wrong
than just the one

the examiner tried
to pin me on.

My memory,
Grandfather laments. *It's not*
what it was.

the verdict

We
wait. Father
and Grandfather
and I, along
with Sow Fong
and others. Wait
to be landed
or rejected.

I come to the end
of my sixth month
in detention.

Sow Fong and I
play Ping-Pong, cards, the game
with the ball and two goals
in the yard. We don't
see Yukiko again
on her bench or find
any more letters from her
beneath the shrub.

Good riddance!
says Sow Fong,
and I find a sense

in which I can agree with him
wholeheartedly.

I was not
the hero of my own story.
I was the villain
of another's.

I play more Go
with Grandfather, learn
to better attack
from strength, reduce
to four stones
the handicap between us.

Sow Fong asks me
in a quiet moment, *Teegee,*
what if we don't
get in? I imagine
returning to my home
in the village, my mother
meeting me at the door
where we said
our goodbyes.

Was it
too big? she asks me,
but I reply, *The*
whole world
is bigger.

One morning
after breakfast,

the verdict comes, for us
before Sow Fong:

Father and I
will be landed.

Grandfather
will not.

enough

This
is absurd! This
can be appealed.
We win most appeals,
you know, though they
can take some time.

Yen Yi and the Association
are gathered
around us.

How
can they land two members
of the same family and reject
the third? Did they accept
two tellings of your paper story
but not the third? Did it not
occur to them
that the oldest man among you
might have the weakest memory?

Father asks if an appeal
would require a lawyer
and how much
a lawyer might cost.

Don't worry about it,
says Yen Yi. *There are landed*
Associations in the city,
long established,
that can help. We are not
without power
in this country. We have
a foothold.

Father asks
how long an appeal
would take, if he and I
would have to stay on the island
while it happened or if Grandfather
would have to stay
alone.

Yen Yi begins to list
the people
we should contact,
measures
we can take.
Then:

No.

Grandfather
stands among us.

I will go back.
I shouldn't be here
in the first place. My son
is dutiful,

a good son,
and did not refuse
when I asked to come,
though I can do no work
and would only be
a burden to him. I only
wished to see
the new world
and the future.

I have seen
enough
of both.

promise

Grandfather plays Go with me
every chance I give him, happily
analyzing our games,
replaying famous battles
of the past for me, and showing me
sophisticated tactics
I'll probably never get good enough
to employ.

He's talkative
at meals, asking Sow Fong
about his family and his plans, laughing
at his jokes (even the ones
so lame, he can't possibly
understand them or he would not
be laughing).

Between our games and meals,
he spends his remaining hours
going around and around
the walls, reading
and rereading the poems.
I realize one day
that he stops at the same spots
every time around, that he must

have favorite poems by now that he's
revisiting exclusively,
like an inveterate reader
flipping to bookmarked pages
of a well-worn book.

I follow him one day
to find out
which they are.

The west wind ruffles my thin gauze clothing.
On the hill sits a tall building with a room of wooden planks.
I wish I could travel on a cloud far away, reunite with my wife and son.
When the moonlight shines on me alone, the night seems even longer.
At the head of the bed there is wine, and my heart is constantly drunk.
There is no flower beneath my pillow, and my dreams are not sweet.
To whom can I confide my innermost feelings?
I rely solely on close friends to relieve my loneliness.

And on the same
stretch of wall:

I have infinite feelings that the ocean has changed into a mulberry grove.
My body is detained in this building.
I cannot fly from this grassy hill,
And green waters block the hero.
Impetuously, I threw away my writing brush.
My efforts have all been in vain.

It is up to me to answer carefully.
I have no words to murmur against the east wind.

The next poem
stands near a window
with a view of the bay. I imagine
its writer doing his pacing
right here,
where he would later
record those moments.

Pacing back and forth, I leaned on the windowsill and gazed.
The revolving sun and moon waxed and waned, changing
again and again.
I think about my brothers a lot, but we cannot see one another.
The deep, clear water casts reflections as waves toss in sympathy.

I look out the window
at the distant, everlasting waves. I'm feeling
the sadness of these poems
in my chest. Grandfather
moves right on
to the next.

In the quiet of night, I heard, faintly, the whistling of wind.
The forms and shadows saddened me; upon seeing the landscape,
I composed a poem.
The floating clouds, the fog, darken the sky.
The moon shines faintly as the insects chirp.
Grief and bitterness entwined are heaven sent.
The sad person sits alone, leaning by a window.

Now upstairs,
says Grandfather,
but I stop him.

Grandfather, are you
unhappy?

He looks
surprised.

No, Grandson.
I'm quite content.

But
the poems,
I say, gesturing
along the wall
of woes.

The poems
are good,
he replies.

The other day,
I try again, *the day*
we learned our fates. You said
you've had enough
of the future.

He pauses
a moment, then
laughs.

Grandson! I said
I've seen *enough.*
This place? The guards?
The powers
that move them? Even
these poems? They
are the present, soon
to be the past.

The future?
he continues,
turning to face me
and taking me
by the shoulders.
I see the future,
too. Enough of it
to know it's full
of promise.

a bet

Father is writing
a poem!

He's carving it
into a wall!

He asked permission
of the Association,
and it was granted.

Has he ever
even *read* a poem?

He works on it
all day with Grandfather,
the two of them huddled
on Grandfather's bunk.
When I ask to see it, he snaps
that it's not ready.
I've never seen him
nervous like this, like a child
rehearsing a part.

What
is he writing?

It could be
anything! says Sow Fong.
The Resistance, the riot,
the attack by the soldiers.
You getting busted
by the Association.
Yen Yi joining them. The guy
who hung himself. What
haven't we seen?

I'm not so sure
that Father sees events
like these, outside himself.

Maybe he'll write
about the poor "accommodations"
and how he overcame them
through long
and focused study.

Maybe he'll recount
his years of preparation
and expense to make
our journey even possible.

Then I realize
that whatever
he writes about, he's sure
to say something
about jabbing the awl,
and I make a bet with Sow Fong
to that effect.

still

On the day
that Father's poem is ready,
he stands at a wall with Grandfather,
cutting his composition
into the collected memory
of all who have passed
through this place.

A crowd
gathers around him
to witness
and support.

I stand with Sow Fong
at the edge of the crowd,
unable to catch
even a glimpse
of the words as they're written.

Father steps back. He consults
with Grandfather, who nods
and pats his back. They move to stand
beside the finished poem, Father grimacing
and fidgeting but Grandfather
smiling. Father proceeds

to recite the poem but in tones
unlike his usual voice, too low
and halting for us
to hear.

The crowd
around him murmurs
uncertainly. There are
puzzled looks, and then
a laugh. Has Father
written something terrible?
Embarrassing? But now
there are sounds
of delighted surprise as well,
and men are shaking his hand.

The Association quiet the crowd
and, facing Father as a group,
commend him
for his contribution.

He thanks them, his voice
restored to its normal strength,
for their leadership and guidance,
Grandfather for all that
and more. He turns to the crowd
and wishes good fortune to all
and their families, in all
their endeavors, here
and in the homeland.

The crowd applauds
and begins to disperse,

with those in the back
moving up to get their looks
at the poem they were unable
to hear. Sow Fong and I
finally reach it.
I read it aloud to him,
and when I'm done,
we can only
stand in silence.

> *I raise my brush to write a poem to tell my dear wife,*
> *Last night at the third watch I sighed at being apart.*
> *The message you gave with tender thoughts is still with me;*
> *I do not know what day I can return home.*

Newb,
breathes Sow Fong. *Your father*
is a stud.

why

Father and I
are scheduled for release
tomorrow.

Sow Fong and I
say our goodbyes.

How
could they land
a loser like you when I
was questioned first,
three times! Did you pay
some kind of bribe? Was that
what you did
the day you supposedly
talked to Boocher?

That's right, I tell him,
and I ratted you out
while I was at it. You have
no hope.

I know, he says, *I*
know: I'm hopeless.
But seriously: you'd better

be there on the dock
to welcome me to America
when I arrive.

You bet, I say,
but then: *I gotta*
seriously ask. (In case
I never see him again.) *Why*
did you pretend
to follow Yen Yi if you think
he's such a bore? Are you—
The momentousness
of the question rises
up my throat. I have to
swallow it back down before
I can resume. *Are you*
the spy?

I've never seen
my mocking friend
guffaw like he does
at that. He doubles over
laughing, has to
brace himself
against a wall. *Newb!*
he sputters. *Newb!*
There is no spy!

Okay, he continues
after catching his breath. *Okay.*
Maybe there is,
who knows? But Yen Yi
certainly doesn't. It's just

important to him
for there to be the fear
of a spy. To keep
the rabble roused.

He settles down
and goes on
with a crooked
smile: *And that*
is why I follow him.

wonder

In all
my future days,
I will never encounter
a greater wonder
than what Sow Fong
goes on to tell me, what
I'll always think of as
his creed.

Yen Yi
is a persuader,
a man with power
over other men.
He can attract them,
rally them, make them believe
whatever he wants. And that
makes him more likely
than anyone else
in this rabble to someday
strike it rich.

I'm disappointed.
Is that all
Sow Fong has been about
from the start? I try

to express support.
I tell him, *Just*
jab the awl,
huh?

No! Wrong! Your father
has no clue! No
real ambition.

He's so excited now,
I barely
take offense.

All he wants
is the wealth
of a wealthy man.
He's going to work hard,
save his pennies. Gain
for himself and his family
a nice house
with a servant or two
and whole rooms
just for guests
or knickknacks: The dream
of Gold Mountain!
The dream of just about
every man here.

But listen! He lowers
his voice, as if we were sitting
in the echo chamber
of the late-morning lavatory. *This*
is what I *want: not*

the wealth of a wealthy man
but the wealth
of an emperor.

They have them here.
Dozens, maybe
hundreds of them,
not just one. Not just
one king at the top
of the mountain but a club,
a cadre, a coterie of men as rich
as any man in history.
Each with not a thousand
but a million times the wealth
of the average
clueless grunt.

And how
do you gain entry
into that club? Not
through hard work
or wise investments.
Not through study or skill
or by saving your pennies.

Not
by "jabbing the awl."

You get there
by persuading others,
as many as you can,
to put you there. By
persuading them that

even having such a club
is essential or inevitable, and not
a totally
made-up thing.

That's
what Yen Yi
has the power
to someday do.
A million-to-one throw
he has a better chance of hitting
than decent, frugal,
hardworking men
like your father
or like you.

I almost
laugh out loud, but instead
I tell him earnestly: *Yen Yi*
doesn't care
about money. And am struck
by Sow Fong's reply: *What*
Yen Yi cares about, what he's
so good at persuading men
to hand over to him,
is power.

I don't know
what to do with this
except to insult Sow Fong
and deal
the next hand of cards.
I think, *In this,*

the Western year of 1924, I've now
officially
heard it all.

I laugh to myself all day
at the thought of men,
not one but dozens, maybe
hundreds, roaming this land
with the wealth
not of a wealthy man
but of an emperor
in their pockets.

But in my bunk, this night
before the ferry
will be conveying us
to that land, I remember
John Brown's lines
about the house
of gilded cards,
and wonder.

the far shore

We board the ferry
for San Francisco.

Grandfather
comes with us, but he
will not
be getting off
with us. The ferry
will take him
to another dock,
where he'll be loaded
onto a ship
that will carry him back
to China.

On the water
once more, I think
of the ocean we crossed,
the long leagues
like a rope we climbed,
hand over hand, up a mountain
not of gold but stone
and dust and,
at surprising moments,
glimpses

of the wide world
around us.

The boat is sputtering
to a stop, the doors
are opening
for some of us,
and Father is standing
with his arms linked
with Grandfather's, their heads
nearly touching
as they whisper final words
to each other. Father
is stooping
to lay his head
on Grandfather's chest,
he, too,
a son.

Then Grandfather is taking me
by the shoulders, telling me
he'll miss our games of Go. *Teach*
Kow Loon, I tell him. *Tell her*
—tell Mother—everything
about this place: the poems
and the powers, the Association
and Yen Yi, the Resistance
and the seven-foot man.
Tell her the future
you see, that I
will see her someday
in it.

And then
we're standing,
Father and I,
on the dock, our luggage
at our feet, finally
and truly landed,
but for a few minutes more
still intent on the past,
our backs to the land
to which we've been
admitted, our gaze
on the ferry turning back
into the bay.

Grandfather stands
at the rear of the boat,
a hand held out, not
in a gesture
of farewell but as if
to say, "Fare forward."

I will,
Grandfather. I
will jab the awl, follow
my father's every rule
of thumb, work long
and hard to make a life
in this new land, but also
I will Resist. I will look
for the arrival
of Yen Yi, look up
the landed Associations
but also John Brown

as he asked. I'll connect
with all The People
in their groups like stones
on a hostile board; we'll fight
to see we are never
surrounded.

I'll look for Sow Fong, too,
however rich or powerful
he might become. Because
he is and will always be
my first friend
in this land. We'll always
come to each other's aid, griping
and hurling insults, without
condition and in truth.

The ferry disappears
around a curve
of the coast.

Are you ready?
asks Father.

I nod.

We turn
from the bay to take in
the streets and structures rising
from the docks, the faces
of every shade in motion
like a thousand clashing currents
churning the ocean

of the new world
before us.

Above us:
an empty sky,
the morning moon
long gone, the stars
as yet unseen (but which
I know are there, beyond
all counting).

I plunge
into the churn,
propelling myself, crossways
to the currents, toward
the far shore
of what will be.

HISTORICAL NOTE

I've tried my best to accurately convey the realities of Chinese immigration through Angel Island in the 1920s. However, this novel is ultimately a fictional story. Though many of its events and characters were inspired by the station's actual history—there really was a self-governing Association, for example, and a radical political organizer who rose to a leadership position, and a seven-foot-tall man who wrote a poem on the walls, and riots for better conditions, and suicides, and a kitchen worker who was beaten by detainees who suspected he was a spy—they're still my own creations and are not meant to portray any specific person or event from the past.

The main characters in this novel would have thought and spoken in Cantonese. However, I've rendered their dialogue and the narration of my protagonist in standard, sometimes very casual, idiomatic English so that they can sound to you like they would have sounded to one another.

RESOURCES

To learn more about the Angel Island Immigration Station:

- *Island: Poetry and History of Chinese Immigrants on Angel Island, 1910–1940*, Second edition, edited by Him Mark Lai, Genny Lim, and Judy Yung (University of Washington Press, November 2014): this is the best book for learning about the station, its history, and the experiences of those who passed through it. (Make sure you get the second edition or later.) It contains translations and the original Chinese of all the poems that have been recovered from the walls, as well as a collection of oral histories told by former detainees.
- The Angel Island Immigration Station Foundation website (aiisf.org): this is the official website of the Angel Island Immigration Station Foundation, containing photos, virtual 3D tours, write-ups of the station's history, and information about how to visit.

To learn and play the game of Go:

- Way to Go (playgo.to/index.html#/en/intro, which you can get to more easily via this shortcut: AuthorFreeman.com/Go): this is a great interactive introduction to the rules and first principles of the game.
- OGS, the Online Go Server (online-go.com): there are many online Go servers where you can play live games against other people, but this is the one I usually play on (my username is deyala).

ACKNOWLEDGMENTS

Thanks and love to:

- the California Department of Parks and Recreation for giving me permission to visit the Angel Island Immigration Station while it was closed to the public during the Covid pandemic;
- the station guides, especially John Clagett, who answered my many questions and pointed me to numerous resources;
- Triton Baduk and Nick Sibicky, two Go YouTubers I follow, who reviewed my Go-related content for accuracy and impact;
- fellow critique group members Michelle Hackel, Nadine Takvorian, and Trish Henry, who oversaw the birth and shaped the development of this novel;
- poet Genny Lim for her invaluable translations of the Angel Island poems and the University of Washington Press for their permission to reprint some of these translations from *Island: Poetry and History of Chinese Immigrants on Angel Island, 1910–1940*;

    Note: One of the poems I quote ("My life at an impasse . . .") was not recovered directly from the walls of the station but recorded by a detainee. That detainee's account of his days in the station, along with the poem he recalled, was translated by Charles Egan. Another poem ("At times, the barbarians . . .") came not from the walls of the Angel Island station but from the walls of the building where detainees were housed before the Angel Island facility was built, and was translated by Marlon K. Hom. The rest of the poems I quote, along with all the poems recovered directly from the walls of the Angel Island station, were translated by Genny Lim.

- my father, Thomas (Ng Tin Sheung, 1913–2012), who made the life I live possible by undertaking the journey to America in 1938; and
- my sister, Karen (Ng Kow Loon, 1947–2004), who of all the people who had a hand in raising me is the person I grew up to be most like.